The Iron Relic
Book I: The Crossing

Bobby Hundley / James Stevenson

HOT
4 chapters a week

ON THE BOARDS PUBLISHING

On The Boards Publishing

1005 East Las Tunas Blvd, #236

San Gabriel, CA 91776

Editor: FirstEditing.Com

Illustrations by Kyle Trott

ISBN-10: 0986300616

ISBN-13: 978-0-9863006-1-5

Library of Congress Control Number: 2014959231
On The Boards Publishing, San Gabriel, CA

Printed in the United States of America.

Visit The Iron Relic Book Series on the World Wide Web at

www.theironrelicbook.com

DEDICATIONS

To my papa Henry for inspiring me to dream, my nanny Isabel for being the example of self-less love, my mom Virginia for always encouraging me to challenge myself and never give up, my father Bobby for giving me faith, and my wife Kristin for your patience, support and love. – Bobby Hundley

To my parents, Dallas and Rita, and my siblings Teresa, David and Joe for the lifetimes of love and support. – James Stevenson

BOBBY HUNDLEY / JAMES STEVENSON

Chapter 1.

Faith lies in the evidence of things unseen.

Doctor Adam Calhoun, a thirty-six-year-old oncologist with wavy black hair, kind brown eyes, and a strong sturdy frame that easily supported his muscular six-foot-tall body, slowly navigated his black 1996 Honda Civic EX 4-door sedan up the winding, ancient oak-lined drive towards the residence of his great-grandfather, billionaire philanthropist Henry Calhoun. The car was a gift he had received the day of his high school graduation from his great-grandfather for graduating with honors from Collinwood Preparatory Academy. The vehicle had remained in pristine condition despite being almost eighteen years old, a testament to Adam's personality. He was raised surrounded by wealth but was never once served with a silver spoon. He learned the value of hard

1

[handwritten marginalia: only people who are super rich can afford money can't buy]

[handwritten marginalia: More character building]

work, the importance of pride of ownership and, more importantly, to have a greater value of and priority for the things that money can't buy.

Adam glanced up through the windshield, blades of sunshine slicing across his sunglasses as he peered at the majestic canopy blanketing the way. The leaves had already begun to crinkle and change color ahead of schedule, bursting into a kaleidoscope of yellows, oranges, reds and greens. Adam fondly thought of a quilt he'd been given by his great-grandmother Florence when he first came to visit his great-grandparents' property almost thirty years earlier. Florence had given Adam the quilt to comfort him on that first night he stayed with them; a night he would never forget as long as he lived.

Adam recalled her sweet voice easing his sadness as she told him that the quilt bore the warmth of all those who loved him, including his mother. "Your auntie, your mommy, your grandma and I all worked together on this quilt. Your mommy stitched this part right here when she was about your age," his great-grandmother said as she pointed a delicate finger towards an embroidered peach butterfly on one of the squares. She then wrapped up the young teary-eyed Adam in the quilt and held him tightly as he snuggled up to her chest. "Whenever you find yourself missing your mother and in need of a hug from

character building always feels same

her, just wrap this quilt around you and imagine her soft arms embracing you. You will feel her love, mark my words," she'd whispered, using the warm, angelic tone that only a grandma possessed. It was as though her wisdom in years confirmed the truth of her words to Adam.

where's dad?

A warm glow filled Adam's heart as he remembered his great-grandmother's words but as he continued to drive under the shade of the trees the warmth gradually dissolved into a recognizable grief. His heart tightened and sank with the same somber feeling he had experienced as a child that first day he was driven up this woodsy path. His mother had died tragically in an *H. Potter* accident and the grieving young Adam was sent to live with his new guardians; his great-grandparents. Now almost thirty years to the day, Adam was traveling up this path for perhaps the last time, ready to experience the pain of loss once more.

The tunnel of trees gave way suddenly to a clearing, revealing the unmistakable triangular facade and hand-crafted brickwork of a sprawling, three-story 1932 Tudor *rich* Revival mansion. Adam navigated his car around the circular cobblestone drive past a series of dark luxury vehicles, and parked directly outside an elegant stained-glass bay window featuring a motif of the archangel

3

Michael casting Lucifer from heaven. He glanced over at the window, taking note of the shadows cast by the people inside the room. This was the audience he was dreading. He took a deep breath, exhaled and unclicked his seat belt.

Inside the mansion, behind the stained-glass window was the library, covered in hardwood from the floor to the high vaulted ceiling. The library felt more like a museum, with historic artifacts throughout, some of them in glass cases, some of them out in the open. Artworks, which included *The Adoration of the Magi*, a tempera and gold on wood by Giovanni di Paolo and *The Annunciation*, an oil on canvas by Luca Giordano, lined the wall. Most were thought to be reproductions, but some of the works drew questions of origin. In one far corner of the room was a simple residential chapel seemingly designed for one; complete with a crucifix mounted to the wall, a serving altar and a single wooden pew. Stacks of papers and journals covered the dark mahogany desk pressed against the bottom ledge of the bay window.

In the center of the room there was a king-sized bed where billionaire philanthropist and the world's oldest living person at 119 years young Doctor Henry Calhoun was resting, surrounded by his immediate family and his doctor, Rose Powell, a beautiful young physician with

4

auburn hair and green eyes. Her skin tone and delicate facial features hinted at an Eastern European heritage.

Doctor Calhoun's face was surprisingly full of spunk for being 119 and gave the impression of a man fifty years younger. He was of Irish descent and built like one of the ancient oaks that lined his driveway. Henry's pride and joy, a silver crucifix pendant, hung around his neck on a simple chain necklace. The room was cautiously silent as the occupants, Henry's family members, watched Doctor Powell prepare to inject medication into Henry's intravenous drip. As she reached out for the drip, Henry suddenly raised his hand to intervene.

"Leave it alone," he said in a gruff but polite tone.

Doctor Powell gently replied, "This will ease your discomfort."

"Discomfort lets me know I am still alive," Henry said with a cracked smile. "Please, no."

Doctor Powell refrained from administering the pain medication and put all of her medical apparatus back into a dark leather medicine bag. Henry turned his attention to the somber faces of his family members, who all appeared to be lacking any kind of jovial spirit whatsoever.

"I'm disgusted," Henry suddenly blurted out.

"Sorry, Gramps," his granddaughter Helen said,

stumbling for an appropriate response. "I, I, I…"

"Stop stuttering and calm down, my Helen doll," replied Henry in a firm but moderate tone. "I asked for one thing today and that's it. An extra-large Sacci's pizza with black olives, mushrooms, Dublin cheddar and salami; and instead I get tears, silence and a new catheter. Today is not turning out to be all I had hoped. Now will someone please tell me who was responsible for ordering my pizza?"

Jordy, Helen's youngest son at twenty-eight years old, a tall, thin, malnourished-looking boy, released an anxious chuckle.

"Is this funny to you, Jordy?" Henry spouted, drilling his youngest great-grandson with a look of disapproval.

"No, Gramps," Jordy whispered, lowering his head.

"Well, at least someone is laughing," Henry uttered to himself then turned his attention back to Helen. "Helen, if you wish to remain executor of my will, then I expect to see an extra-large…"

Helen turned anxiously to Jordy. "Jordy, order Gramps his pizza, now. My credit card is in my purse in the foyer. Go. I told you to do it earlier."

"I didn't know where your purse was," Jordy rebutted.

Helen's quick boil temper ignited as she scolded Jordy. "Boy, I am going to knock the stupid out of you if you do not get that pizza ordered right now!"

Jordy recoiled and started for the door.

Henry shouted after the denounced young man, "And tell them they better be here within an hour or I might not be!"

Jordy scurried out of the room as Henry laughed heartily to himself, thoroughly amused by his own comment. Helen looked down, attempting to control her thoughts about the whole situation and began pacing the room. Henry noticed the thumping sounds of his distraught granddaughter's heavy pacing and found himself feeling guilty for the emotional stress Helen was experiencing. He watched her lovingly, and gently began to pucker whistle a familiar lullaby.

The tune drifted its way into Helen's soul, easing her body slowly to a standstill. She closed her eyes and began to recall her childhood and all of the fun slumber parties she'd had at the home of Gramps and Grams. Back then Henry told all of his grandchildren, before they were old enough to know any better, that he was a world champion whistler and had even won an Olympic gold medal by whistling that very tune. The lullaby had such a soothing effect on the children that it would lull them to sleep without fail. A tear drop slipped from Helen's eye, which she immediately wiped off her face using the cuff of her blouse.

Henry said to her in a sympathetic tone, "It's okay to look sad, my Helen doll, but this is not the end, only the beginning." *what does he mean*

Helen nodded in acknowledgment as she walked up to Henry, taking his hand in hers. Pete, Helen's younger brother at fifty years old, glanced up from his newspaper and smiled at them. Pete had remained seated quietly the entire morning in a black cloth recliner near a statue of the Virgin Mary holding the baby Jesus. Across from Pete, playing a game of solitaire on a portable electronic device was Sean, Helen's oldest son at thirty-two. He appeared unfazed by everything that had been going on around him until the sudden knock on the library door.

The entire room turned its attention to the door which slowly crept open as Adam popped his face into view. Henry perked up instantly, released Helen's hand, and reached out with both arms towards Adam. The eye contact between Adam and Henry told the tale of their strong bond, which went well beyond great-grandson and great-grandfather to more of a son and father.

Henry beamed as he greeted Adam. "Adam! Finally, someone with a sense of humor shows up to brighten the day of a passing old man!"

Adam shook his head, rolled his eyes, and smiled at

his great-grandfather's abiding sense of tragedy as he shoved down the fear that this may be the last time the two would speak. "Hey, Papa. I'm glad you could hold out long enough to see me," Adam said with a playful smirk.

"Come over here and give me hug before my doctor sticks something else into me," Henry said with a hint of sarcasm.

Doctor Rose Powell looked up from her chart a bit aghast and unsure of how to reply. Adam turned his attention to Rose to inquire about Henry.

"How's he doing?"

"I'm dead as a duck," Henry interjected.

"Apart from the obvious?" Rose replied rhetorically to Adam, and then playfully turned her attention to Henry. "I think it might not be a bad idea to take some fluid samples. Ship them off to the Smithsonian."

Henry laughed and pointed at her as he said with a smile, "I'm going to miss your sass, Rose. You're one of a kind. It's not every day a man asks to see an angel before he dies and gets sent one to be his doctor."

Doctor Powell blushed as she closed the folder containing his charts. She glanced over to Henry and gave him a bright smile and a charming crinkle of her nose. Adam carried on walking over towards Henry, nodding and greeting his other family members along the way.

alteration *dev.*
character

Helen stood stoically by Henry's side and then politely backed up a few steps from Henry's bed to make room for Adam.

"Hi, Aunt Helen," Adam said as he leaned over and gave her the expected hug. He then turned his attention to Henry, who grabbed him by the arm and pulled him in for a hearty bear hug that one would not have expected from a man of his age.

"I'm glad you showed up before the vultures started picking my bones," Henry said to Adam while the two embraced.

"And I'm glad to see your humor is still intact," Adam replied.

Henry noticed Doctor Powell checking his urine bag. "Doc Rose, I'll bet you didn't know the word humor originally referred to our bodily fluids." *interesting*

humor

"Yes, I did, and sometime around the sixteenth century, it became used to describe one's state of mind," Doctor Powell playfully responded, quite proud of herself.

Henry nodded his head towards Doctor Powell as he said to Adam, "Adam, did you know that Doctor Rose Powell is single? And when I say single, I mean single and looking for some handsome, successful young man who might also be in the field of medicine to sweep her off her feet."

Doctor Powell's blush turned from a soft pink haze into a deep ruby red. Embarrassed, she quickly turned away and went on, rushing to finish her final checks.

"Okay, Papa, that's enough accosting of Doctor Powell," Adam said wryly.

Henry peered off in the general vicinity of the remaining family members and said, "Would my dear family please give me a moment in private?"

Concerned and wanting to be useful, Helen awkwardly blurted out, "Do you need another bedpan, Gramps? I can get it for you."

"No! I want to be alone with Adam for a moment," Henry asserted.

Pete calmly rose from his chair and reached over to Sean, lifting him up by his arm. "We'll be right outside, Gramps," he chimed as he ushered Sean over to the door. Doctor Powell had already gathered up her belongings.

Helen reluctantly walked over to the door, all the while looking back over her shoulder at Henry and Adam with a suspicious eye. Henry quickly took notice of her and, with a flick of his hand, said, "Close the door. I don't have all day."

Helen stood in the doorway like a defiant child as tears welled up in her eyes from the slight of Henry's dismissal. Pete calmly placed a relaxed but solid hand on

Helen's mid back and helped guide her out of the library.

After ushering Helen, Sean and Doctor Powell out of the library, Pete slowly pulled the heavy solid library door closed behind him.

Just outside the library door, in the brightly lit hallway, was an antique walnut drop leaf end table smartly arranged next to a solid antique hand-carved walnut settee upholstered in soft cream chenille. Sean, still focused on his game of solitaire, plopped down on the settee as though he was tired, bored and ready to spend the rest of the day in a bar. Doctor Powell retreated to the living room and relaxed on the leather sofa, gazing at the fire in the large brick-mantled fireplace.

Helen wedged herself between Pete and the library door, hoping to be able to hear the private conversation going on between Adam and Henry. She pulled her shoulder-length hair into a pony tail with her hands, taking in a deep breath, and released the hair upon exhale. It was a habit that she had had since childhood and it signaled to everyone who knew her that she was nervous and displeased. Pete took a step back to give Helen some room, and gave her a disapproving eye roll. Helen locked eyes with Pete and glared.

"What's so special about Adam?" Helen asked. "I'm the one in charge of Gramps' will and I don't get to have a

Adam's father

special conference with him. I get shipped out into the hall and told to order that stupid pizza."

"You know he's always had a soft spot for Adam, ever since his father left him," Pete said in an attempt to calm Helen's nerves. "Gramps took it upon himself to treat Adam as a son. Then Mary passed away, and the poor boy only had Gramps. Gramps raised him. It's only natural he sees him more as a son and less as a great-grandson."

jealous

"Adam's not his son," Helen snapped back. "He's his great-grandson. We're the grandchildren. Gramps should be closer to us."

who's

"Helen, there's nothing to say that if Mary hadn't died, we still wouldn't be out here in the hall while Gramps was having this conversation with her."

Helen considered this for a moment then said, "What could they possibly be talking about? All the funeral arrangements have been made. Gramps has had this moment planned down to the last detail for thirty years."

"Exactly. Gramps has always had a plan for everyone. When Mary died, Gramps made it his own personal mission to see that Adam had every opportunity that the rest of us were given. You can't blame Adam for the misfortune of losing a mother and a father. Do you think Mary planned to die in that boating accident and leave a

Adam's mom

six-year-old at home?"

"Irresponsible. You didn't see me going sailing with small children at home. Mary, Mary—even her name was his favorite. How could any of us compete with that?"

"Hey, what are you all doing out in the hall?" Jordy asked, disrupting the conversation while walking back from the kitchen.

Helen muttered in a low defeated tone that seemed unfamiliar to her sons, "Mind your own business."

Jordy handed the cell phone to Helen and sat on the settee next to his brother. "The pizza will be here in about twenty minutes."

*****

Adam hovered next to Henry's bedside in the library as Henry carefully removed the necklace from around his neck by pulling it over his head. The silver crucifix pendant shone as he rubbed the round turquoise stone embedded on the back of it with his thumb. He looked upon the pendant lovingly as one might gaze upon a life-long friend as they reached the end of their days together and come to peace with that fact. Henry held the pendant up with his left hand towards the direction of the private chapel and crucifix, which was directly in Adam's line of sight. The pendant reflected a beam of light across Adam's cheek and forehead.

"This old necklace has been one of the great miracles of my life," Henry began fondly. "The other miracle was the birth of my daughter, your grandmother Mae. I had hoped my obituary would say I'd died a great-great-grandfather, but there isn't any chance of that, is there?"

Adam shook his head. "I would have to at least start with finding a girlfriend," he smirked.

"I might know a few suitable candidates," Henry said with a charming lilt.

"Papa, it's not an election."

"I told you Doctor Rose is available."

"She's a colleague. No. Isn't there anything else you want to talk about other than my love life? It's not that significant."

"The loves of our lives are the only significant things in this world, Adam."

Adam thought on this for a moment and then replied, "I don't have time for a relationship in my life right now."

"Time runs out faster than you think," Henry said simply, "so you better start making some time. I want to give you something, but first, you have to make me a promise."

Adam instantly became leery of his great-grandfather's request and his expression gave his feelings away. He'd heard this tactic from Henry before.

Henry noticed the young doctor's lack of enthusiasm. "Don't give me that look. You're not a teenager anymore," he chided. "I need you to promise me that what I say, you will take seriously, whether you believe it or not."

Adam nodded. "OK, fine. I promise."

Henry extended his left hand, which held the necklace and crucifix pendant. "I want you to have my necklace," Henry said with a touch of sentimentality. "There's a great story behind this necklace. I came into possession of this piece during one of my digs in Turkey, back in 1919. This portion here," Henry turned the crucifix pendant over to reveal a small clasp attached to the turquoise stone on the back, "flips open to reveal a small chamber inside the pendant. Inside that chamber rests the broken tip from one of the Holy Nails that pierced Christ's flesh."

Adam let out a loud sigh. "Come on, Papa. Do you know how many of these stories there are out there, and how many of them you were the source of? They are all over the internet. You can bid on this type of stuff. Propaganda."

"You are absolutely correct," Henry retorted. "Most of it is a smoke screen for the truth, but what I am telling you is one hundred percent honest, which is why you are the only person I can leave this information with. This chamber does contain the missing tip of one of four nails

16

that punctured Christ's flesh and will forever be stained in the blood of our Father's only son on Earth. I know this as a fact because it saved my life. I took it from a piece of the True Cross itself. The end of the nail was broken off, embedded deep inside the olive wood."

"The cross was lost and has never been found, you said so yourself," Adam skeptically replied.

Henry, frustrated by Adam's resistance, clamped his hands down and began to retell the tale of the Holy Nails. "Two nails —"

"Yes, I know, Papa," Adam said, interrupting Henry. This was a story he had heard Henry tell a hundred times before. He recited the tale back to him. "Two nails were used by Helena, mother of Constantine the Great. She had one forged into a helmet for her son and the other forged into a bridle for the emperor's horse, to protect them in battle. The third was cast into the Adriatic Sea to calm a storm and the fourth was turned into part of a crown known as the Iron Crown of Lombardy."

Henry took Adam by the forearm, pulling the young man into him. He stared into Adam's eyes with a look of force, conviction and fear that Adam had never seen before from his great-grandfather and would likely never experience again. Henry suddenly rested his head back on his pillow and calmly said, "That is correct."

Adam gently took Henry's hand in his and reassuringly said, "You're just tired. Let's talk about something else."

Henry stared back at Adam and in a fractured voice said, "That is correct, except for the fourth. The fourth was not turned into part of a crown. The fourth is a nail with a curiously blunt tip, hidden away, deep in the Vatican."

"Papa, if what you are saying is true, don't you think this necklace should be passed along to someone with a little more..." Adam paused as he searched for the right word so as not to offend his great-grandfather.

"Faith?" Henry mused.

"Or a museum, or the Vatican?"

"I have given enough to museums, and the same goes for the Vatican," Henry said as he took Adam by the hand. "I'm not forcing you to become a believer, Adam. I'm asking for your help."

Adam nodded apologetically. "Anything you ask."

"Thank you," Henry whispered. "Thank you. I only ask two things. One, keep this a secret. Two, when the time comes, pass this along to another deserving individual in need of healing."

"What makes you think I am in need of healing?" Adam said defensively.

"We all are in need of healing, Adam," Henry said wistfully. He pulled Adam down to him and embraced his great-grandson. "I love you, kid."

"I love you too, Papa," Adam said with a tear in his voice.

"There's one more thing." Henry leaned towards Adam's ear and began whispering.

Adam listened intently, this time held captive by whatever his great-grandfather was sharing. It was as if Henry's words were flowing through Adam's eyes and molding into his facial expressions. After a few moments, Henry slowly lay back, leaving Adam with a quizzical look on his face.

Adam was dumbfounded. He stared at his great-grandfather and said, with a question, just a name. "Alroy Byrne?"

Chapter 2.

Nestled deep in the heart of downtown Chicago was a sparsely furnished high-rise office lined with bookshelves that were filled with rare books any bibliophile would covet. A single rich mahogany desk faced the wall of windows that overlooked the entire Chicago city skyline. As the sun began to dip below the city's buildings, marking the onset of early evening, a fifty-inch widescreen television set mounted on the wall to the left of the desk came on, just in time for the Channel Eight News.

On the screen was a young woman, roughly thirty years old, with dark brown hair. She wore a dark pinstriped suit jacket over a patterned blouse, and a silver horseshoe pendant hung from a small silver chain hugging her neck line. The open jacket and low neck line

of the blouse revealed enough cleavage to be interesting to men, but not enough to be unprofessional. She was standing in front of a white wooden sign with black lettering which read BISHLAM FUNERAL HOME. She spoke into a microphone encased in plastic with a large eight stenciled on it.

"Doctor Henry Calhoun, renowned philanthropist, archeologist and the world's oldest living person, has sadly passed away in his home at the age of 119. He was surrounded by his family during his final hours. Doctor Calhoun, born in the year 1894, was often the center of controversy, accused of using stem cells, among other techniques, to achieve his world-record age. Doctor Calhoun will be remembered globally for his work with children's charities, bringing vaccines to under-privileged communities and saving countless lives. The John C. Trever Museum of History will be honoring Doctor Calhoun with a ceremony, dedicating a wing in his honor and presenting the Doctor Henry Calhoun Exhibit for the public to view free of charge. The family will be holding a private ceremony later this week. I'm Christina Hernandez with Channel Eight News."

The television suddenly clicked to black, turned off by the remote control in the hand of a dark figure seated in a high-backed tufted black leather office chair behind the desk. The dark figure placed the remote control down on the desk and picked up a cell phone with his left hand. He pressed one button on speed dial while lifting the phone to his ear. On the man's left hand ring finger was a large golden ring with the emblem of a slaughtered lamb resting on a scroll with seven seals made of encrusted rubies. Two words were spoken. "It's time."

Chapter 3.

A line of people entered the large two-story white-sided colonial home that had been converted into the Bishlam Funeral Home. Many mourners were expecting to see and pay their respects to Henry Calhoun; however, they discovered a closed casket memorial service. In addition, the funeral home director, a mousy little man by the name of Elam Bishlam, informed guests that they would not be allowing time for testimonials. The small reserved sign placed on the corner of the front pew saved the front row for the Calhoun family. Seated in the front pew were Pete, Helen, Jordy, Sean, and Adam.

"Gramps didn't want anyone testifying about him," Pete leaned over and whispered to Helen. "He said if anyone had anything to say about him they could've said it while he was alive. God knows he lived long enough."

Helen shot a sharp glance of disapproval at Pete for breaking the silence.

"Somebody check and make sure it's not full of bricks," Sean whispered to his brother Jordy.

"I wouldn't put it past Gramps to do this just to get some peace and quiet," Jordy whispered back.

"Hush!" Helen snarled at her sons a little too loudly to not be heard by everyone in the first six rows. "Show some respect."

Mr. Bishlam walked to the podium and tapped the microphone attached to the back of the mahogany structure. Satisfied that his tapping was properly amplified through the six small speakers mounted along the left and right walls in the room, he gave a nod to Pete, signaling that all were seated and it was time to begin.

Pete stood and approached the microphone stand. He cleared his throat while pulling a piece of paper from his jacket pocket. Pete read the eulogy—a poem Henry had selected years ago, 'September 1913' by William Butler Yeats.

As Pete read the title, the year 1913 for some reason triggered Adam's curiosity. "1913, 1913, 1913. What was the significance?" Adam thought. Then it hit him. Henry had whispered to him, "Look to September 1913," right before he mentioned the name Alroy Byrne. "But why?"

Adam pondered as his curiosity turned to frustration.

After reading the poem, Pete folded the piece of paper and quietly sat back down in his seat. All was still for a moment, and then one by one, all of the mourners began to leave. After the room was emptied of all but the Calhoun family, Pete turned to Adam and handed him the folded paper.

"Henry wanted you to have this, although I can't imagine why."

***

The exterior of the Bishlam Funeral Home glowed peacefully in the sunlight as the pall bearers marched the ornate gold leaf casket out of the chapel and loaded it into the solid black hearse that had been waiting in front of the funeral home. A moment later, the back door of the funeral home opened and four men who worked for the funeral home carried out a simple wooden casket and loaded it into a plain white station wagon. The station wagon drove around slowly to the front of the building, past the hearse carrying Henry Calhoun's casket, and out the circle drive onto the main road.

The hearse containing Henry Calhoun's casket pulled out of the driveway followed by an army of limousines, Mercedes, Bentleys and other luxury vehicles being escorted by a police motorcade. The procession continued down the road toward Our Lady of the Angels cathedral where Cardinal David O'Leary was waiting to greet the family and lead the burial mass.

Our Lady of the Angels had been built to replicate the early Romanesque style of the Church of St. Michael in Heidelsheim, Germany. The cathedral was built on the same symmetrical plan as the original, with two apses, characteristic of Ottonian Romanesque art. The interior of the cathedral was the image of its original counterpart as well, including the wooden ceiling and painted stucco work. It was a double-choir basilica with two transepts and a square tower at each crossing, just like St. Michael's. The west choir, however, did not contain a crypt as the original one did.

Cardinal O'Leary, a plump, jolly white-haired man who resembled Saint Nicholas without the beard and mustache waited patiently until the congregation had filled the church. Extra chairs had been placed in the aisles, and still some were forced to stand against the back and side walls. The choir sang "On Eagles' Wings" to begin the event. The traditional Catholic Requiem Mass continued with prayers, or The Office of the Dead, followed by a performance of the Absolution of the Dead to end the ceremony. This was a series of prayers to God requesting that Henry's soul not suffer the temporal punishment in purgatory due for the sins that were forgiven during his life. After the absolution, the casket, family members and a few close friends were taken to the burial site in the well-manicured grounds of the Heavenly Acres Cemetery.

Adam's face reflected in the glossy cherry-wood casket as the light from the morning sun bathed the burial site of Henry Calhoun. Water droplets gently splattered across his image on the casket as Father Fletcher, Henry's longtime friend and confessor, blessed the casket with Holy Water. The Calhoun family and friends, dressed in dark mourning attire, encircled the final resting place of Henry Calhoun. Each person in attendance solemnly held a white rose as a beautiful singer gracefully serenaded them with a powerful rendition of "Ave Maria." During the song, attendees formed a line leading to the casket so they could pay their last respects.

Adam watched them as, one by one, they approached the casket and placed their white rose on the top of the polished lid. A simple tribute for a man revered by so many, Adam thought to himself.

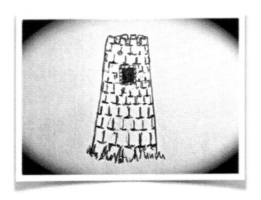

Chapter 4.

Peter Calhoun-Mitchell's home, a lavish estate that locals and a few magazines had dubbed the Mitchell Castle, stood proudly atop a large hill, overlooking the ten-acre property that Peter called his yard. The large brick eight-bedroom mansion included five fireplaces, museum quality art and décor. The five-story watch tower built on the south-east end of the original structure was chiefly responsible for the home's nickname.

The large house was quiet, filled as it was with only a handful of family members and close family friends. A buffet food line had been set up in the main dining hall, and was catered by several individuals wearing white dress shirts and dark slacks.

In the corner of the foyer that led into the dining hall, Helen was waging a heated conversation with her younger brother, Pete.

"Gramps wore that necklace day in and day out every day of his life," Helen said, almost foaming at the mouth. *angry*

Pete responded defensively. "I didn't take it; you didn't take it. Maybe it was placed in the lockbox. Did you place his necklace in the casket's lockbox by mistake and forget about it?"

"No! The necklace was on his body when we were at the house so that only leaves the funeral home and whoever was at the house when Gramps died. There was you, me, Adam..."

"Sean, Jordy, his doctor, Dr. Powell," Pete recalled as he noticed the doctor speaking to Adam near the vegetable trays.

angry

A split second of fury flashed across Helen's eyes as she stared Doctor Powell down. "Her. It had to have been her," she spouted as she marched straight for Doctor Powell.

Pete knew he had better intervene quickly before Helen made a fool of herself by causing a scene. He called after her, "Helen, what are you doing? Don't start accusing people..." but it was already too late.

Helen charged up to Doctor Rose Powell, pointed her bony index finger at Rose's chest, and demanded, "Give me my grandfather's necklace!"

Rose, stunned by Helen's sudden attack, searched the faces of Pete and Adam for help.

Helen bulldogged Rose again in an even louder and more demanding tone, "His necklace. You were in the room with him before it went missing. You signed his death certificate."

Rose, struggling to compose herself, professed to Helen, "I do not understand what is going on here. You all were in the room with me when I pronounced the time of death."

Pete positioned his body in between Helen and Rose in an attempt to cool the situation. Guests were now starting to take notice of the disruption and they turned their attention towards Helen. Pete raised his hands gently to the various guests, signaling that all was well and for everyone to go back to their conversations.

Rose inched closer to Adam and out of Helen's striking radius. She was not willing to take any chances. Grief had a funny way of affecting people, she thought to herself.

Pete calmly turned to Rose to apologize. "Dr. Powell, I'm so very sorry. My sister is having a hard time dealing with our grandfather's death. The stress sometimes gets the best of her."

"I understand. I'm very sorry for your loss," Rose

replied solemnly.

Helen fired back at Rose as if Rose's comment had struck a cannon's fuse with a torch. "Don't patronize us. You know where his necklace is," Helen snarled.

Pete interjected in a commanding voice, "Helen, enough is enough. Jordy, take your mother out for some air."

Helen muffled her voice and appeared to be grinding her jaw down to dust as it took all of her strength to remain silent during Pete's reprimand.

"Mom, come on. You're getting worked up. Did you take your medication?" Jordy carefully prodded as he took his mother by the arm.

"Let go of me," Helen demanded yanking her arm away from the young man and storming out of the room.

"Wow, it's a party now, huh?" Pete said, half joking. "Go make sure your mom is okay. I don't want her burning down the house," he said to Jordy in a more serious tone. Jordy nodded and went out after Helen.

Rose took several deep breaths in and out to settle her nerves. Adam politely touched her elbow, attempting to provide support but careful to keep the gesture from being interpreted as more than what it really was.

"Rose, I'm sorry. I'm not sure what just went on here," he said.

31

Pete replied nonchalantly, "Helen is just worked up because she couldn't find Gramps' favorite necklace when she closed the casket. It was a family heirloom that he wanted to be buried with. It's really no big deal. She gets a little extreme sometimes. Don't take it personally."

Rose nodded in understanding as she said, "I'm really sorry. I am. I wish I knew where it was and could help with the situation."

Pete turned his attention to Adam. "Adam, how are you holding up?" he asked.

"Better than expected. Look, I've got to run. I have some patients to check on," he said as he noticed the time on his watch.

"Eli?" Pete asked with a sense of familiarity.

"Yea," Adam answered, averting his eyes.

"How's he doing?" Pete asked, noticing Adam's evasive behavior.

"Same old Eli. Chased off three hospice nurses so far." Adam chuckled, hoping to sidestep the core of the conversation. He found himself dodging more and more questions pertaining to the health of his best friend these days.

Pete sensed Adam's discomfort with the conversation and smiled at his nephew. "Let's meet this week for coffee—in between your busy schedule. Just call me—

doesn't matter what time. There's that twenty-four-hour diner not far from the hospital. I don't sleep much nowadays," Pete said as he placed his arm around Adam's shoulder in a half hug.

"I will," Adam said before turning his attention to Rose. "Dr. Powell, thanks again." Adam extended his hand as a professional courtesy. Rose shook his hand politely.

"I'm sure we'll run into each other in the halls," Rose said as Adam headed for the foyer.

Adam glanced back over his shoulder at Rose and, for the first time, he saw in her what his great-grandpa Henry was talking about. She was a stunning woman; and not just physically. She also had an enchanting, calm but strong air about her. He allowed his guard to fall and his mouth broke slightly into a smile. Rose smiled back as she locked eyes with Adam for a brief moment that would chronicle the first shared spark of interest between them.

Chapter 5.

A modest but neat yellow wood-sided single-story house stood on a small plot of land in the middle of a long line of two-story homes situated along a narrow street. Adam, still wearing his black suit and tie from the memorial service, parked his car in front of the small house and climbed the eight concrete stairs that led to the front door. Without knocking or ringing a doorbell, Adam let himself in through the white metal storm door. Once inside the home, Adam walked through the front room, noticing a pink sweater draped over a chair in the kitchen. He walked past the kitchen and entered a bedroom toward the back of the house.

Eli Taylor, Adam's closest childhood friend, was lying in bed, suffering from terminal cancer. His close-cropped blonde bangs were pasted to his forehead by sweat. Eli was noticeably underweight. His hospice nurse, a Filipino woman in her forties, who was wearing light green scrubs that had pictures of the Sesame Street character Oscar the Grouch all over the smock, was attending to him. A bright white name tag announced her name as Terry. Having just changed the linens on Eli's bed, Nurse Terry was lifting a white plastic laundry basket containing the dirty linens when Adam knocked on the bedroom door and walked in.

"Hey, bud. Nice of you to come dressed for my funeral," Eli quipped, a jovial tone in his voice.

"Oh, I'm sorry. I just came from Papa's memorial," Adam said shyly.

"Oh man, that's right. I'm sorry. I saw some of the news clips earlier," Eli said, losing his jovial tone.

"How's Nurse Terry treating you?" Adam asked.

"To be quite honest, not good," Eli said, glaring at her disapprovingly. "She wants to give me a catheter but I told her, contrary to popular belief, that that is not the way to a man's heart."

As Nurse Terry walked out of the bedroom, she turned towards Eli, and, not showing any emotion towards him, simply stated in a monotone, "You pee the bed again and I'm putting you in diapers." She closed the door with her elbow and exited the room.

"I like it when you talk kinky!" Eli shouted after her.

"Be careful," Adam warned. "You don't want them to send another replacement. You might get a no-nonsense, scruffy male nurse, who won't be so ... loving."

"As long as his hands are soft," Eli said with a grin, and then his demeanor turned more somber. "I am really sorry to hear about your great-grandpa. He was a very good man."

Adam walked over to the wooden two-toned dining room chair, noticing the chair was exactly in the same spot he had put it the last time he visited. It hadn't been moved since.

"He had a lot of years to be thankful for," Adam commented quietly as he took the chair and placed it closer to the bed to sit next to his friend. Adam noticed that Eli had turned his gaze downward to his hands, which were clasped over his chest, rolling rosary beads between his fingers. "Sorry," he whispered.

"No. Don't be. He was fortunate. Do you know what the odds of living to be one hundred are?"

Adam shook his head and said, "I need to brush up on my *Jeopardy* knowledge."

"Odds are pretty good actually; around twenty-three percent. I did an internet search of it. Of course, to live to 119 that I don't think there's a percentage for. Your great-grandpa ... to say that that dude looked good for his age is an under-statement. Wish I knew his secret. Is it true you injected stem cells from cord blood and mixed dried placenta in his green tea?" Eli inquired.

"What are you talking about? No. And you'd never catch him drinking green tea. Strong black tea, "cha" as he called it, with lots of milk."

"So that's his secret. Cha."

"There's an old Irish proverb my papa used to quote to us: 'God made time, but man made haste.' He told me the only reason he lived so long was because he needed more time to enjoy his cha."

"And your thoughts on the subject?"

"He was a hearty Irishman."

"You ever watch any of those ghost shows on TV?"

"Occasionally."

"I just got hooked watching one of them where celebrities talk about their ghostly encounters and I started thinking if my spirit hangs around this world after I'm dead, then I'm definitely shacking up with Kate Upton. That's my new dream—to haunt Kate Upton." Eli thought about the Hollywood bombshell. "What do you think the odds are of that?"

"I think every day on this Earth is precious because that may be all that we get."

"You can be a real killjoy sometimes, you know that? No appreciation for the unknown factors in life."

"I think my views give me a stronger appreciation of what's around me."

"Is that why you became a doctor? To have a stronger appreciation for everything around you?"

"I became a doctor to help give people as many days as possible."

"Well, for your sake, let's hope you got your genes from Henry's side of the family. Can you imagine the things he must have seen? Jim Thorpe playing professional football before there really was pro football. Insane. Speaking of which, when is football season going to start already? Every year it feels like it takes longer to get through the pre-season."

"Are you that eager to watch your Cardinals get beat down?"

"Don't diss my birds. I haven't seen that much out of your team the past few years, unless you count leading the league in penalties." Eli laughed then changed the subject of conversation. "How'd your date go, with 'Sassy' Selma?"

"I didn't go," Adam revealed as he cleared his throat.

"Ouch, dude," Eli taunted while feigning a slight chest pain. "I worked hard to get you that date. Do you know how much time it took for me to set up an online profile for you, answer all those questions for YOU and then get you matched with that very hot-"

"Twenty-year-old sorority girl, who thinks some boy band from Canada is da' bomb and has as her life's goal to learn to make Belgian waffles because she's one-fifth Belgian. Yea, that isn't exactly what I'm looking for."

"I thought you liked waffles."

"I'm perfectly capable of finding a date."

"When?"

"When I'm ready for one."

"You go out on fewer dates than a Himalayan monk with scabies. As your relationship advisor, I'm here to remind you that you are throwing away the best years of your life. The grey hairs are going to kick in soon and I'm not just talking about the ones on your head. Women don't find that attractive."

"I'll file that advice away in the memory banks of 'I'm not interested'."

"I'm serious, man. You haven't been on a serious date since Tara died."

An awkward silence filled the room and Eli immediately regretted mentioning Tara's death. Adam had still not recovered from losing her; he may never fully recover.

"Can we change the subject?" Adam urged, fighting back the impulse to raise his voice and yell at Eli. Of all people, Eli should know that Tara was an off- limit topic for discussion. Instead of getting furious with his friend, however, Adam chose to remain calm and keep the visit peaceful. "As I recall, we have an unfinished chess match." Adam walked to the dresser where the small magnetic chessboard rested atop a light-brown bamboo breakfast tray. He carefully lifted the tray from the dresser, allowing the folding legs that were underneath the tray body to drop down into their standing position. "You didn't cheat and move any of the pieces, did you?" he asked as he placed the tray over Eli then return to his seat.

"Please. I don't have to cheat to school you in chess. Bring it on," Eli said as he pushed himself up into a more comfortable sitting position.

"OK, but I can't play long. I've got another patient I want to check on." Adam reached out with his right hand and placed his fingers around the black bishop, contemplating a move.

"Wow, I must be really sick if you're going to make it that easy for me to win," Eli teased, mocking Adam into taking more time to examine the board.

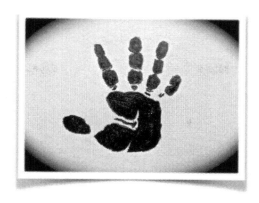

Chapter 6.

Twenty-five minutes after being defeated by Eli in chess, Adam walked quietly down the hallway of Hope Hospital's Simmons Children's Ward. The walls were brightly colored in primary colors that seemed to glow vibrantly under the fluorescent lights at night. One section of the wall was decorated with the painted hand prints of children. The hand prints were outlined and then custom-decorated by the child whose hand it represented. One hand had a pretty pink bow painted across it with a dove perched on the finger tips. Other hand prints were colored in with flowers, some with superheroes, another with a smiley face, and some were just painted in. Adam stopped near the end of the section and reached out, placing his hand over a print that was especially tiny. The child who'd made it could not have been any older than three or four years old. It was stamped in ink on the wall instead of painted. After a moment, he continued on down the hallway.

Adam walked over the top of a series of rectangles that formed outlines for the game of hopscotch. The rectangles ran down the center of the hallway floor. Adam walked over to the nurses' station and greeted the nurse behind the counter. Deborah Walker, a twenty-eight-year-old blonde-haired, blue-eyed nurse in the oncology ward was sitting behind the counter working on a patient's chart and hadn't noticed Doctor Calhoun walk up to the desk. His voice startled her and caused her to jump in her chair.

"How's young Mr. Collins doing today?" Adam said.

"Oh, Dr. Calhoun, I didn't notice you there," Deborah said with an awkward embarrassment that could lead one to believe she had a small crush on the doctor. She quickly recovered her composure and went back to being all business. "Mr. Collins' lab results from his biopsy should be ready. I'll check with the lab and notify you either way. Other than that, he has been asking for a checkers rematch."

Adam smiled for a moment then his demeanor turned more serious. "And how's our little trooper in twelve?"

"Her condition hasn't changed. She's showing no

signs of improvement. Bag's still empty," Deborah responded.

"Thanks. Page me if anything changes." Adam tapped the counter with his fingertips, chewed the inside of his mouth slightly then turned to walk away.

He walked down the long corridor and paused at the elevator. It was late in the day and had he been working, his shift would have ended an hour ago. He pressed the down button and waited for a moment, but then he reconsidered the trip to the doctors' lounge and decided to take the stairs to the cafeteria instead. Adam took a detour on the way down to the cafeteria and stopped by the third floor. He walked out of the stairwell and turned to his right then made an immediate left and walked through the double doors that separated the main hallway from the maternity ward.

Adam stopped in front of the nursery's large glass viewing window and leaned against the wall. On particularly rough days, Adam often found himself making the journey down to this section of the hospital. He loved the sense of new life, and seeing the babies lying in their cribs was extremely soothing to him. He could clear his mind and concentrate on whatever it was that was bothering him, whether it had to do with a certain patient or a family matter. Today it seemed to be both.

Henry's funeral had seemed rather anti-climactic for Adam. His great-grandfather had been such a huge and important part of his life that Adam felt like too little had been done for him on his funeral day. A pang of regret crossed his heart. His friend Eli's declining condition also weighed heavy on Adam's mind. Eli wanted Adam's friendship more than his assistance but Adam felt obligated to give equal portions of both. Regardless of his efforts, though, Eli's condition was not improving.

Nor was the condition of his young patient in room twelve. The teenage girl he had been treating for most of her young life was succumbing to her illness. Adam felt as though he had spent too little time with each of them today, and yet the day was so full of heartache and depression, he felt like he couldn't afford a moment more. The young doctor couldn't remember a time when he had felt so helpless, so useless. Adam leaned against the wall and gazed into the little sleeping faces and tiny curled fists and tried to let the stress of the day fade.

Two young men came into the hall and stopped in front of the large window. One of the men, a very proud new father, was introducing his younger brother to his new nephew. The joy in their voices snapped Adam out of his trance. He pulled himself off the wall and walked back to the stairwell, descended two more flights and

44

headed toward the cafeteria.

As Adam walked down the long corridor to the hospital cafeteria to pick up his dinner, his footsteps echoed in the emptiness of the quiet hospital. He allowed his thoughts to drift and settle on the relaxing clicking sound his leather-soled shoes made on the immaculately polished tile floor. Adam turned the corner and entered the cafeteria. The cafeteria was empty except for a couple of orderlies drinking coffee. Lydia, a plus-sized African-American woman in a purple smock, was behind the serving counter, reading a magazine and humming what sounded to be "Amazing Grace" to herself. She glanced up from the magazine and let out a smile as big as Alaska upon seeing Adam.

"Good evening, Dr. Calhoun!"

"Good evening, Lydia."

"You're running later than normal. I thought maybe you'd decided to cook for yourself once." Lydia lay the magazine down on the counter, open and face- down so as not to lose her place, then reached below the counter to a lower shelf and retrieved a Styrofoam to-go box. She chuckled lightly to herself. "Today was spaghetti; I gave you extra meat sauce, like always." Lydia smiled a huge smile as she handed Adam the container over the glass sneeze guard that separated them.

"Thanks, Lydia, you're a saint," Adam said as he felt the weight of the container. She had indeed added extra sauce. Adam turned and walked out of the cafeteria, heading home for the night.

"I know," she yelled after him, smiling and picking up her magazine to continue her reading.

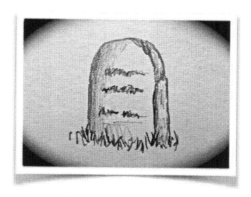

Chapter 7.

Two grave robbers with pen-sized flashlights snuck up to the grave of Henry Calhoun. The two men were brothers; Hiram and Horace Grey, from Chicago, Illinois. Hiram, at forty years old, was the larger and leader of the two. His tall forehead and long crooked nose overshadowed his sunken chin and curved down corners of his mouth, and gave him a naturally sinister look. The man stood at a hulking six foot seven inches, and although being 280 pounds would put him in the obese category on the BMI scale, most of Hiram's weight could be attributed to muscle. At first glance, one would mistake him for a professional football player, not a professional petty thief.

Horace was a thirty-three-year-old miniature version of his brother, though his dark brown hair had not receded as far from his forehead as his brother's, his nose had not been broken as many times and the corners of his mouth were turned more upward. Horace also stood a modest five foot seven inches tall, and weighed in at a miniscule 135 pounds. Horace's major distinguishing feature was his ears, which appeared to be two sizes too large for his head, thus the nickname Mouse which he had carried with him since childhood.

The two thieves were dressed all in black, with ski masks pulled over their faces to hide their identities. They lit up the marble tombstone with their flashlights to inspect the name on the headstone.

The ornate stone read: "Until we meet again, in a place beyond the soft blue skies, where our souls will glide and our hearts will rise, to the peace found in God's own eyes. Henry Calhoun. December 25, 1894 – August 28, 2014."

Horace tugged at his mask around his mouth. The knitted yarn was unraveling, causing him to furiously puff air out of his lips and spit in order to keep from swallowing the dark blue strands.

Hiram turned to him and smacked him on the arm. "Stop doing that. It's getting on my nerves."

"Then you shouldn't have given me this crappy mask. It's like our grandmother knitted this back in the 1800s,"

Horace grumbled.

"Shut up, Mouse. We have a job to do," Hiram said with a heated intensity to his gruff voice, which sounded like gravel turning in a cement mixer. "Down!"

Hiram threw Horace onto the ground like he was a stuffed animal. Their bodies sunk slightly into the fresh-turned soil as a security guard in a green golf cart, with an emblem of a willow tree encircled with the name Heavenly Acres, drove down the walkway towards the grave. The security guard was diligently spot-checking the grounds as he drove. He slowed his golf cart down slightly approximately twenty yards away from Horace and Hiram and watched as the sprinklers kicked on in that section of the cemetery. An orange cat with black and white stripes bolted across the grass at the sudden shock of the water. The security guard laughed to himself. This would be the only form of excitement or entertainment he would get that night, he thought to himself as he pressed the accelerator.

Horace had what felt like a pound of fertilized dirt churning around in his mouth from being shoved to the ground by Hiram. He struggled to control his gag reflex as the dirt pushed back against his tonsils, choking him. Unable to contain himself any longer, Horace popped his face up from the ground and coughed out a face full of soil.

49

Hiram grabbed Horace by the back of the neck with one huge hand and shoved his face back down into the dirt as the security guard was now almost upon them.

Horace's cough sent a strange echo in the cemetery that caught the security guard's ear. He stopped his golf cart on the path several yards from the gravesite, picked up a high-powered flashlight from the seat next to him, clicked it on and shone it over Henry's gravesite. Horace squirmed, struggling for breath, as Hiram firmly held him down. The beam of light skimmed the air above the heads of the two grave robbers, barely missing them.

The security guard stood silently for a moment and looked in all directions. If a pin dropped, he would hear it. The grounds remained silent. Satisfied, the security guard clicked off his flashlight and drove on, continuing his rounds. Hiram released Horace's neck. He gasped for breath as he hacked out chunks of saliva- infused dirt.

"You could've killed me," Horace said, struggling to clean his mouth.

"Hurry up. We have less than an hour before he drives around again," Hiram growled.

The two men began digging up the grave as fast as they could, moving faster and faster with each shovelful. Each heap of dirt tossed aside brought the men inches closer to their prize. Horace thrust his spade deep into the soil and felt his arms buckle as the end of his spade ricocheted in front of him. A hollow thud was heard. Horace had driven his spade into the top of the coffin.

Hiram shoved Horace to the side and dropped on his knees beside the coffin. He used his hands, as if driven by a violent ambition to clear the remaining dirt from the top of the coffin. "Tell us what we have, Johnny," Hiram said in his best game-show-host tone as he shoved a crowbar into the lock.

Horace climbed out of the hole and nervously glanced around the cemetery. SNAP! The lock broke. Horace turned his attention to the coffin, staring in anticipation as Hiram opened the casket lid. Hiram stood over the casket and then hurled his crowbar out of the grave, barely missing Horace's head.

"Hey! That's the second time you almost killed me tonight!" Horace scolded, his patience nearing the end.

"Empty. Gimme a hand and get me out of here," Hiram spewed.

"What do you mean, empty?"

"It's empty. There's nobody! No one is home. Empty, dummy."

"Impossible."

"Climb on down here and see for yourself if you don't believe me. The only body in this grave is mine," Hiram hissed. "Maybe they cremated the guy and spread his ashes."

"I was at the funeral. They buried him," Horace affirmed.

"Did anyone see the body in the casket?"

"No, it was a closed casket. Pry open the lock box. Look inside."

Hiram removed a screwdriver from a tool kit attached to his belt. He turned on his flashlight and placed the end of his flashlight into his mouth as he climbed inside the empty casket. He twisted the screwdriver into the crack of the lockbox above the lock and then leaned back against the head of the casket. He cranked his right leg up to his chest and slammed his foot down onto the end of the screwdriver, causing the lockbox to crack open. Inside the lock box was a small card. The yellowish paper, roughly the size of a business card, had a message typed on one side. "No one can serve two masters, for either he will hate the one and love the other, or he will be devoted to the one and despise the other. You cannot serve God and money. Matthew 6:24."

"The boss isn't going to like this," Hiram whined to himself.

"Hurry up, come on. We need to cover this site up and get the hell out of here." Horace started tossing dirt on to

52

Hiram, who had just started climbing out of the grave.

"Watch it," he snarled.

After filling the grave with dirt, the two grave robbers went back to an older model white minivan that they had parked in the side street across from the entrance to the Heavenly Acres Cemetery. Hiram sat in the driver's seat, Horace in the passenger seat; a cell phone with the speaker phone function selected lay on the console between them. There was a slight tremor in the large man's voice.

"I swear, boss. There wasn't a body in the grave. We're not lying. We're not trying to keep it for ourselves," Hiram said fearfully.

"He's right, boss. We checked the lockbox, everything. Nothin' was in there," Horace chimed in, trying to soothe the situation.

A deep, resonant bass voice came over the speaker phone. "You had better hope no one got to that grave before you, for both of your sakes."

Horace sensed his future wellbeing hanging in the balance as he gingerly reassured the voice on the other end, "No, no one came here before us. I've been here since they put the coffin in the ground. You want us to take a picture of the empty coffin?"

The voice answered in a disgusted tone, "No, idiot.

You better pray you dug up the right coffin. If his body wasn't in that grave, then someone in the family knows what is going on. I want you two to get eyes on everyone in that family. Find out who has got that necklace. I want eyes on E-V-E-R-Y-body in that family."

"We won't let you down," quivered Horace.

"You better not," warned the voice.

Chapter 8.

Adam entered his sparsely furnished apartment, carrying his spaghetti dinner in one hand and his keys in the other. He went through the same routine he followed every night. He tossed his keys into the key dish on the side mantle in the foyer then walked to the bedroom. He put his cell phone and wallet on the nightstand next to a picture of Tara; the picture he'd taken of her with his cell phone one day as they were picnicking in the park. It was the first cell-phone photo he had ever taken.

They had been out having an impromptu picnic. Tara loved experiencing spontaneous moments, and Adam would often oblige by taking her out on this type of outing. It was a beautiful late summer afternoon. The leaves on the trees were just starting to lose their vibrant green color, readying themselves for the upcoming fall change of color. Tara's auburn hair glistened in the sun as her brilliant bright blue eyes reflected the day's energy back to Adam. Her burgundy red sweater was the only indication that the air was cool. At the moment Adam snapped the photo, Tara thought he was reading a text from a friend on his phone. It was truly a candid photo that revealed the love she had for him. Now, next to her beautiful smile and windswept hair, in the lower left hand corner between the frame and the glass that protected the photo, was her funeral card.

The faded blue card portrayed the image of Jesus hugging a woman. They appeared to be on a cloud with the faint image of an angel hovering above and behind them. The inscription on the back of the card was etched in Adam's memory forever. It said:

In Memory of Tara McEntire

June 20, 1978 – April 8, 2004

LORD, make me an instrument of Your Peace.

Where there is hatred, let me sow love;

Where there is injury, pardon;

Where there is doubt, faith;

Where there is despair, hope;

Where there is sadness, joy.

Adam carefully took his stethoscope from around his neck and laid it in front of the picture, taking a moment to gaze at it. He mouthed the words, "Honey, I'm home."

Adam left the bedroom and continued to the kitchen where he heated the spaghetti on a ceramic plate in the microwave and then sat at a small table in the corner of the kitchen in front of a window. As he placed a white napkin from the table onto his lap, his hand brushed the silver crucifix in his pocket, and he was reminded of his great-grandfather's necklace. Adam took it out of his pocket and held it up to inspect the silver crucifix in the light. He turned it over and examined the turquoise stone, considering whether to attempt to open the secret chamber or not.

Outside Adam's home, a shadowy figure was standing on the sidewalk, looking at the silhouette of Adam holding the small crucifix. He pressed a button on a cell phone and held the phone to his ear.

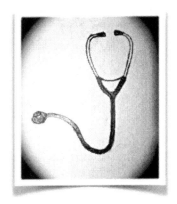

Chapter 9.

The next morning, Adam woke up to the buzzing sound of his alarm clock. He showered, got dressed and went to the hospital, stopping by the cafeteria for a cup of coffee and a plate of scrambled eggs, two links of sausage and a glazed donut, as he did daily. Then he went to the children's oncology ward and walked straight to room twelve.

Adam peered through the doorway and gently knocked on the door. His patient's parents, Isabel and Dave Martinez, greeted Adam, doing their best to smile and put on a happy face. Their daughter Claire, a young teenage girl battling leukemia, was a ray of sunshine; positive, outgoing and cheerful in spite of her condition. She was the type of teenager who won your heart with a smile and her charismatic personality instantly made you feel like you had been longtime friends. Even with oxygen tubes in her nose, she mustered up a vibrant smile as she greeted Adam.

"Hiya, Doc," Claire said.

"How's our trooper this afternoon?" Adam asked as he shook hands with Isabel and then Dave.

"She seems to be doing better today," Isabel answered, an uncertain tone to her voice.

"Mom, Dad, may I confer with my doctor in private for a minute?" Claire asked politely.

Isabel nodded. "Sure, honey."

Dave leaned over Claire's side and gently kissed her forehead, a look of sadness evident on his face.

"Cheer up, Dad," Claire said, trying to console him as she lightly bopped him on the chin with her fist.

Dave gave his daughter a toothy smile, revealing who Claire took after when it came to her wide bright smile. Hand in hand, Dave and Isabel slowly walked out of the hospital room.

"Confer," Adam said, impressed. "I see you've been reading that daily word calendar I gave you. How's my favorite teenager?"

"I have my bags packed to head home," Claire announced in the same optimistic tone that Adam was accustomed to hearing from her.

"That's the fighting spirit," Adam responded, checking the nurses' notes on Claire's chart.

Claire suddenly took on the demeanor of a girl wise beyond her years. "Give it to me straight, Dr. Calhoun. I'm not doing so well this time, am I?"

"I'd like to see a little more pee out of you," Adam admitted calmly, referring to the urine bag attached to a catheter hose on the side of the bed. The bag was relatively empty with the exception of a few minor drops.

"It has been three days. My kidneys aren't working, are they?" Claire asked.

Adam paused for a moment as he searched for an appropriate response for her.

"Just give me the truth," Claire continued.

"No. They're not," Adam said, very straight forward.

"The last doctor who checked on me said it was because the infection was so bad. I heard him tell my mom and dad in the hallway. He told them that I would most likely go into a deep sleep, like a coma. That doesn't sound too bad to me."

"Claire, I'm going to keep trying everything I can to get you home."

"Either way, I'm going home, Doc," Claire replied wistfully. "What do you think heaven will be like?"

Adam found himself tightening up at the subject. The

confidence of a stellar oncologist was fleeing, turning him into an unsure friend. He mustered up the best answer that came to mind.

"Where dreams come true," he surmised.

"I like that," Claire said. "Good job."

"Well, thank you," Adam said with a slight chuckle as Claire disarmed his anxiety.

Claire looked up at the ceiling and said, "I had a dream last night where I was covered in colors of music, surrounded by angels—but when I floated to the gates. They weren't golden...they were made of Lego." She chuckled to herself softly. "I half expected to never open my eyes again and just continue on my way but then I woke up with one of the nurses checking my vitals. You know, it is okay that you don't believe in heaven, Dr. Calhoun."

"What makes you say that?" Adam asked.

"Body language. Your pause said everything. Eighty percent of all communication is done through body language," Claire said with a sense of pride.

"You're a very perceptive young lady. You'll make a great doctor."

"Yea, I would have. One of the priests here at the hospital is supposed to come give me the Last Rites. I asked my mom to bring my rosary today but she forgot. I don't blame her. She's kind of stressing out pretty hard about me."

"I'm sure the father will have one."

"It's not the same—I was hoping to hold onto it when I ... cross over, you know," Claire said, disappointed.

"I tell you what, I'll ask some of the nurses and see if I can find one for you," Adam replied.

Claire instantly brightened up and held her hand out towards Adam. "You promise?" she asked.

"I promise," Adam said as he shook her hand, sealing the deal.

Chapter 10.

After finishing his shift, and checking in on a sleeping Claire one last time for the day, Adam went to the doctors' lounge. He was feeling rather defeated by his young patient's deteriorating condition and he needed a moment alone. He entered the lounge and noticed that it was quiet and empty, as he had hoped. The coffee pot invited Adam over with an odor of a semi-fresh brew, although the small volume of coal black fluid in the clear glass pot suggested otherwise. The kitchenette area was clean and all of the chairs were still neatly tucked under the small round tables, hinting that no one had used the room since the night time cleaning crew had been through.

The television in the corner was on and showing an advertisement that Adam had seen before. A red- haired man dressed in all white was shown in vignettes, laying hands and giving faith healings with the words "Second Coming Event" in bold white letters at the bottom of the screen. Adam saw the TV remote lying on the table closest to the door that led to the locker room. He picked it up and aimed it at the television. Just as the faith healer on the screen was mouthing the words, "The Second Coming is upon us, He will reveal himself" Adam turned the television off.

Out of the corner of his eye, Adam noticed he wasn't alone after all. Doctor Rose Powell was sitting on the couch that was against the back wall. She was holding the calendar section of the newspaper in her hands. The headline read, "Henry Calhoun, A Dedication" and there was a large half-page photo of the John C. Trever Museum of History on the front page.

"I'm looking forward to checking out this exhibit at the History Museum," Rose said. "Are you going to see it?" She caught herself. "Of course you are. I'm sorry...."

"Huh?" Adam asked, obviously distracted by his own thoughts and not paying full attention to Rose. "I'm sorry I have ... one of my patients went into renal failure. It doesn't look good."

"How old?" Rose asked, showing concern for Adam's feelings and putting the paper down.

"Thirteen."

"Don't give up. There's always a chance," Rose added.

"Dr. Powell...?"

"Yes?" Rose asked, waiting for Adam to finish his question.

"Sorry. Nothing. Never mind."

"You sure?"

Adam nodded his head. He was going to ask Rose if she would accompany him to the museum dedication, but then he reconsidered. The timing just didn't seem right. Adam turned and walked through the doorway that led to his locker.

"Okay," Rose said quietly to the empty room. She stood up, lay the newspaper on a table and walked out of the break room.

Adam sat on the bench in front of his open locker, trying to gather his thoughts. The loss of his great-grandfather, the scene his Aunt Helen had created at Henry's funeral reception, his best friend Eli's deteriorating health, his job and teenage patient's condition were all on his mind. Adam took off his scrubs, grabbed a towel and headed for the showers, hoping the cold water would help him clear his head. Before he could turn the water on, he heard his phone ringing from his locker. The ring tone told him the call was coming from the nurses' station. Adam dropped his towel and hurried back to his locker to answer his phone. The nurse informed Adam that she had notified the family, and a hospital priest had been called to deliver Claire's last rights. Adam put his phone back into his locker and returned to the shower. There was nothing more he could do.

After his shower, Adam remembered the promise he had made to Claire and went on a search of a rosary. He asked all of the nurses at the nurses' station if any of them had one; none of them did, but one nurse suggested he try the gift shop in the hospital lobby. Adam rushed through the maze of corridors only to find the gift shop closed. He headed back through the maze of corridors, heading to the back exit that led to staff parking, hoping to find a rosary at a nearby store. As he turned a corner, he ran into Doctor Powell, almost knocking her down.

"Oh my gosh!" Adam exclaimed. "I'm so sorry, Dr. Powell. Are you all right?"

"Fine. I'm fine," Rose answered.

"I know this is an odd request, but you wouldn't happen to have a rosary on you, would you?" Adam asked. "I made a promise to my thirteen-year-old patient, and it looks like she needs it right now. The priest has been called."

"I'm so sorry, Dr. Calhoun. I don't."

"That's all right. Sorry again for almost knocking you over. I wasn't paying attention to where I was going."

"I understand. Good luck."

"Thanks," Adam said as he headed toward the exit. He walked out into the parking lot and quickly stepped over to his car. As he reached into his pocket for his car keys, Adam's fingers discovered his great-grandfather's necklace with the silver crucifix. Adam took the necklace out of his pocket and looked at it for a moment. It wasn't a rosary, but he thought at least it was something. He rushed back into the hospital and headed straight to room twelve, Claire's room.

Adam opened the door just as the priest was placing Holy Oil on a table. The Holy Oil would be used in the second part of the ritual, the part referred to as the Anointing of the Sick. Adam quietly folded the unconscious girl's hands around the crucifix as the priest began his prayers. The girl's hands tightened slightly around Adam's and the crucifix then loosened. Her monitor flat lined. The priest continued his prayers as if he didn't notice the noise.

Adam stood in shock, hand in hand with Claire while the priest continued the Lord's Prayer. He lowered his head in resignation. Claire had passed, and Adam knew he must note the time of death. He tilted his wrist to check his watch and at that instant, he caught a tiny glint of light out of the corner of his eye coming from beside Claire's hospital bed. The flicker came from the small drops of pee that had started to drip into her bag.

Adam released Claire's hand and took a step back. Now the silver crucifix was in Claire's hands only, and a steady stream of urine flowed into the bag. A slow heartbeat broke the steady whine of the monitor. The priest took notice of the heartbeat and then fell silent as he stood in amazement, convinced he was witnessing his first miracle.

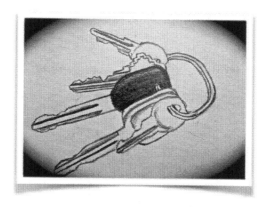

Chapter 11.

On the other side of town, Elam Bishlam, the funeral director of the Bishlam Funeral Home, stood outside the back door of the large colonial home, a large set of keys dangling from his right hand as he pulled the back door firmly closed. Elam flung the keys around his index finger with the appropriate key to the lock landing perfectly in between his thumb and forefinger, an action he had perfected over the past forty years of operating the business. As the key clicked the lock into place, he felt a burning sensation at the back of his skull and then the warm wet rush of blood stream down the back of his neck. His eyes rolled shut and Elam's body fell to the ground with a loud thud, the keys jingling against the pavement.

A gloved hand reached down to retrieve the keys from the pavement then the lock to the back door clicked. The hinges squealed as the door was pushed open. A pair of gloved hands grasped Elam under the armpits and dragged him through the back door into the funeral home.

Elam's eyes opened slightly, just in time to watch the back door close as his stunned body was pulled deeper inside the building. He struggled to move his head towards the direction his body was being pulled and could not decipher if he was seeing double or if his attacker was not alone. Elam closed his eyes and drifted back out of consciousness.

Chapter 12.

Adam removed his backpack from his locker and sat down on a bench in the locker room, still trying to process Claire's seemingly instant recovery. Doctor Rose Powell lumbered through the doorway and approached her locker then noticed Adam, who appeared deep in thought as he stared down at a spot on the floor in between his feet.

"Whatever you did was amazing," Rose commented.

Adam looked up, caught off guard. "I'm sorry," he asked.

"The miracle with your patient. That was incredible," Rose answered in awe.

"I didn't do anything except pray with her," Adam admitted modestly.

Rose smiled to herself at Adam's humility and continued with the faith of a true believer in miraculous works. "No matter what hospital I go to, there's always something medicine just can't explain. You look like you could use someone to treat you to a good meal."

"I usually just pick something up from Lydia in the cafeteria."

"Like I said. Come on, celebrate the victories in life. Grab your bag. I'm not taking no for an answer, Doctor," Rose exhorted as she extended her hand towards Adam to help him up from the bench.

***

The lighting was dim in the Medio Bistro. Many of the chairs were already upturned and resting on the table tops as the restaurant was near closing. A young couple celebrating their anniversary walked by, arm in arm, carrying the remnants of their meal in a dark brown to-go bag. The couple flirted as they swerved past the tables towards the exit. They passed Adam and Rose, who were sitting quietly across from one another as their server, a young college student, did his best to relay the evening's dinner specials.

The server looked up at the young couple and smiled. "Happy Anniversary," he said pleasantly to the couple as they walked past. "We hope you return soon."

The couple barely took notice of him as they left the all but deserted dining hall.

"Our fish special is a wild salmon glazed in a peanut soy wasabi base with a side of wild rice," the young man finished.

"That sounds delicious. I'll have that," Rose stated.

The server jotted down Rose's order and turned his attention to Adam. "And for you, sir?"

"I'll stick to the half chicken and salad. But can you make sure they do not put any of the crushed walnuts on it," Adam replied.

"Absolutely," the young man said as he read back the order to himself quietly. "A half chicken, salad. No nuts. I will get that in for you both right away." He then walked briskly towards the closing kitchen.

Adam took a deep breath and slowly exhaled before looking up at Rose. "I just want to apologize to you in advance."

"For what?"

"In case I'm a horrible date. I haven't done this in a long, long time," Adam admitted, blushing.

"Who said this was a date?" Rose looked at Adam with a serious expression on her face.

Adam's face turned beet red with embarrassment. "I...uh...I didn't mean to imply...I'm..." He began to stutter, trying to find another way of apologizing to Rose.

"Hey, hey, don't have a seizure. I'm kidding." Rose

chuckled, teasing him. "I did ask you out, but only because I've been waiting and waiting and waiting for you to ask me out for a long while now," Rose confessed.

"Really?"

"Yes."

"See. I am no good at this. And I just don't want to turn into that guy who unloads all of his emotional baggage on a first date."

"Trust me. I know more about you than I probably should at this point," Rose jested.

Adam gave her a curious glance. "And how exactly?"

"I was only your great-grandfather's doctor the past eighteen months. He was quite the talker," Rose teased. "Don't worry, mostly good stuff. He talked about your mother, and your fiancée."

Adam looked down at his clasped hands. The subject of his dead fiancée, Tara, was a very uncomfortable one for him, although he did realize that he had to move on with his life.

"I'm sorry, I didn't mean to hit a sore spot." She instantly regretted this slip in conversation. The last thing she wanted to do was to remind Adam of this tragedy and push him away from her.

"No. It's been over ten years now since she passed," Adam murmured. "I guess we can jump to dessert then, huh?" he continued, trying to lighten the mood.

"See? Now I am making you feel uncomfortable and I didn't mean that." Rose took a deep sigh and tried to gaze into Adam's eyes; however, his gaze was still fixed on his hands. "So, about that dessert, what's your favorite dessert of all time?"

"Ooh. Hmm. Vanilla ice cream."

"Seriously?" Rose asked, shocked.

"I'm serious. Plain. An oldie but goodie. What can I say? It's sentimental. Reminds me of my mom."

"No strawberry glaze or nuts?"

"Can't have nuts. I almost died when I was eight. My Papa made me a sundae covered in crushed nuts—the usual walnuts, peanuts. I took one bite and that was it. My body went into anaphylactic shock. All I remember is waking up in my bedroom with Papa beside me. He had a terrified look on his face. That was the only time I think I ever saw my great-grandpa Henry scared."

"Well, I will remember not to bake you any of my specialty peanut butter snicker doodles for your birthday. Anything else I should watch out for?"

"Um, I'm not a fan of heights," Adam replied, finally looking up from the table and meeting Rose's gaze. "Otherwise I'm pretty good. And you?"

"I love all foods. Golubtsy holds a special place in my

heart. No allergies that I know of. I definitely like to jump out of perfectly good airplanes, and doves. I collect porcelain dove figurines."

"What's golub, goloob?" Adam fumbled the pronunciation.

"Golubtsy. It's a stuffed cabbage that my mother used to make."

"Sounds yummy. You can make me that instead for my birthday," Adam stated with a bold charm.

"Oh, that's pressing your luck. I haven't had a boyfriend make it to that point yet," Rose flirted.

"Hot plate!" the server warned as he set down a half chicken plate on the table, effectively breaking the evolving mood between Adam and Rose.

***

After finishing their meal, Adam and Rose continued talking in the brisk night air in the empty parking lot of the Medio Bistro. Their cars were parked a few feet away from each other. A bus boy tossed a series of black trash bags into a nearby dumpster and then walked back into the restaurant through the kitchen's back entrance. He closed the solid metal door to the kitchen behind him and then, abruptly, all the lights on the property went out.

"I think they want us to leave." Adam chuckled as he rubbed his hands together.

"I really enjoyed myself tonight. Thanks for taking me up on the offer." Rose smiled and crinkled her nose as she gazed into Adam's eyes.

The moment froze for Adam as he was suddenly overcome by the sensation of butterflies in his stomach. He became hyper aware of every feature on Rose's face, from her gentle dimples to a tiny scar next to her left eyebrow to a beauty spot below her right eye. Every detail was beautiful to him. It was as if her smile whisked away all the stress from his mind. But was she feeling the same way? Is this the moment I try to kiss her? Doubt and insecurity seeped into his body. Was he ready to date? Was he ready to date a colleague? His life wasn't like the television show *Grey's Anatomy* or even *E.R.* There was none of that drama and excitement, and certainly not the soap opera-like romances of doctors dating doctors and stealing kisses in the supply closets. He lived a pretty quiet, isolated work-life. But was that really the problem aching at his soul or was it the memory of his beloved Tara? He'd never taken the time to experience the grief of that loss.

Tara and Adam were both so young with bright futures when they fell in love. She died less than a couple of months before they were set to graduate from the Washington University School of Medicine in St. Louis.

All of this emotion roared through Adam's mind and body like a riptide, a tsunami of energy that flooded him in what was probably less than a split second, too fast for him to even acknowledge all of the parties involved in the conflict warring inside of him. He was not himself, and perhaps that was a great thing because had he been himself, he most likely would not have been brave enough to utter the words that came next.

"So, about the museum dedication for my Papa Henry. Would you maybe be interested in being my date?" Adam cautiously asked.

"Yes, I would love that," Rose said. She was both surprised and elated that he took the initiative. All she could think of was Adam's great-grandfather Henry telling her that if anyone was going to get Adam to date again, they would probably have to club him over the head and drag him off cavewoman style.

"Great. I'll talk to you more about the details at work this week," Adam said, his confidence growing.

"Definitely. I'm looking forward to it," Rose said as she nodded. She took his hand in hers. "I am really, really glad you came out to dinner tonight. I was afraid I might have had to club you over the head like a cavewoman to get you to go out with me."

"I was that oblivious, huh?" Adam replied with a

smirk.

Rose tilted her head slightly from side to side. "Kind of," she said with a laugh. She took the keys out of her purse. "I should get going. I have an early shift tomorrow."

"Okay. Oh geez. Do I -" Adam anxiously muttered to himself.

Rose grabbed his face and kissed him, and the two embraced for a moment. They stood, eyes closed, inches apart from one another's face.

With his eyes closed, Adam finished his sentence. "I was going to say do I ask for your number now, but what you did works."

"Oh." Rose looked away shyly. She turned back to him and said, "Give me your cell phone."

Adam removed his cell phone from his pocket and handed it over to her. She pressed the touch screen and tapped the contacts icon on his phone. Adam's contacts populated, which was nothing to write home about as there were only four numbers; Eli's, his Uncle Pete's, his great-grandpa Henry's, and Tara's.

Rose noticed Tara's name and looked up. "Are you sure you are okay with this?"

Adam nodded and replied, "I will be. Yes. I am."

Rose lowered her eyes back down to the cell phone

and programmed her name and number into his contacts. She pressed save and handed the phone back to Adam. He opened her car door for her and she stepped inside. Adam gently closed her car door and walked in front of the car, crossing the headlights as he headed to his vehicle. Rose lifted her hand in a delicate good-bye gesture as he passed in front of her. He returned the gesture and got into his car to leave.

Meaning
Peace

Chapter 13.

Elam Bishlam opened his eyes. Slowly the white-tiled ceiling of the chapel in his funeral home came into focus. His head ached badly, and as he tried to pull himself into a sitting position on the floor, sharp pains shot through his rib cage, his right shoulder and his kidneys. He had been beaten badly; so badly, it hurt to breathe. He realized that no one was in the funeral home yet this morning, and he would have to crawl or drag himself to a phone. He gathered his strength as he tried to regain his bearings. He would call 911 and ask for an ambulance first, and then he would call his wife and ask her to meet him at the hospital.

Elam dragged himself along the burgundy carpeted floor of the chapel with his left arm in short slow pulls. Bursts of pain paralyzed him occasionally, and at least twice, he felt that he was about to lose consciousness. Once he finally made it to the closed door that led out to the hallway that would take him to his office and his phone, he stopped and tried to sit himself upright again. When he was half way to a seated position, the door quickly pushed open and hit Elam in the head, knocking him unconscious.

Ruth Samuels, a brassy thirty-four-year-old who had been cleaning for Mr. Bishlam for eighteen years, set her shoulder against the solid oak panel and forcibly pushed the door to the chapel open. Elam Bislam's unconscious body rolled over, allowing a gap between the door and door jamb just large enough for Ruth to squeeze herself through. She slipped her right foot into the room and stepped down, crunching on Elam's right hand. A sudden moan shot up from the floor. Ruth lifted her foot and let out a high pitched yelp much like a coyote's yip at the terrifying shock of seeing the unconscious body of her employer on the floor. Ruth quickly ran to the office and called 911.

It took seven minutes from the time Ruth called 911 for the ambulance to arrive. The paramedics put a neck brace around Elam's neck and then carefully strapped him to a back board. They put the board onto a gurney and wheeled it to the ambulance then sped off to the hospital. The drive to the hospital was quick with the aid of the lights and sirens, but the driver did notice a significant increase in traffic once they got closer to the hospital.

When the ambulance pulled up to the Emergency Room doors of Hope Hospital, the two paramedics quickly got the gurney out of the truck and pushed it into the E.R. Having called ahead, they were met at the door by the triage nurse, Tabitha Philos. She helped transfer Mr. Bishlam onto a hospital gurney and took him to room number six. It would be another thirty-four minutes before an available doctor looked in on Elam. The hospital was a very busy place that day, and anyone not busy was occupied with the murmuring and gossip about the miracle that had occurred the night before.

Down the hall from the Hope Hospital Emergency Room, Adam walked up to the nurses' station to ask about his young patient, Claire. Two nurses were recounting the events from the evening before as if they were in the room themselves. The word miracle was used several times, Adam noticed.

"The priest was giving the patient her Last Rites and she flat lined. Just as the doctor was about to call time of death, poof, she came back," the nurse exclaimed. "Miracles do happen."

"The body works in mysterious ways, ladies," Adam commented as he picked up a file from the desk.

"The Lord works in mysterious ways, Doctor," one of the nurses corrected Adam as he walked away.

Adam walked down the hall and into room twelve. Claire was sitting up in her bed and Adam noticed there seemed to be more color to her cheeks and a light in her eyes that hadn't been there before. The girl's parents were standing over her, beaming with joy and gratitude when Adam entered the room. Upon seeing the doctor, they immediately smiled and tears began to flow down their faces.

"Don't tell me miracles don't happen," Isabel said to Adam as she grabbed the doctor and kissed his cheek.

"There's our fighter," Adam said to Claire, ignoring the miracle comment. "I just wanted to drop in on you and make sure everyone is treating you well."

"Like a celebrity," Dave replied.

"Father Kellen is calling her recovery a divine miracle," Isabel interjected.

"I had faith in you, Doc," Claire said to Adam as she held out the silver crucifix necklace. "I saw you hand this to me last night."

"You saw me hand it to you?" Adam asked. He didn't think there was any way she could have actually seen him hand the necklace to her. She was unconscious and slipping off into death as he placed the silver crucifix into her hand.

"Yea," she replied, "but it's time for it to go back to its rightful owner." Claire opened her hand out flat for Adam to take the silver crucifix necklace.

"You keep it," Adam said quickly. He wasn't sure why he said it, but hearing the words come from his mouth sounded right. He had made a promise to his great-grandfather, but maybe Claire needed the cross more than he did.

"That wouldn't be right of me," she said as she tipped her hand to let the necklace drop to the blanket covering her legs. "Trust me."

Adam picked up the silver crucifix necklace and started to tuck it into his pants pocket. Then he had a second thought, and placed the necklace back into Claire's hand.

"You can give it back to me when you check out and go home. It shouldn't be long. It looks like you're doing just fine. I'll be back later to check up on you."

Claire nodded in agreement. Satisfied, Adam left the happy family alone and continued on his rounds.

Chapter 14.

Adam slowly pulled his black Honda into his drive way and parked. He grabbed his Styrofoam box dinner from the passenger seat and walked to the mailbox and took a quick look inside. The sight brought a smile to his face. The mailbox was empty, making for a nice bonus to a fantastic day. No mail meant no bills.

Adam walked to the front door of his home, unlocked the door, and placed his keys in the dish on the side mantle in the foyer. When he turned to walk to the bedroom, he noticed that there was something different about his apartment. Something was out of place. Out of the corner of his right eye, Adam noticed a mass on his living room floor. It was the cushions from the couch. They had been slashed open with a knife and some of the stuffing had been pulled out. Adam paused for a split second as his brain tried to process the information.

"What the...." Adam started to say.

Two men in dark clothing, their faces covered by black ski masks, jumped Adam from the doorway leading to the kitchen. Adam's Styrofoam dinner box was sent hurling against the wall, spilling grilled chicken breast and rice across the foyer. The hulking Hiram grabbed Adam and held him up against the wall next to the front door. Horace punched Adam in the stomach several times, knocking the wind out of him, and then held a knife up to his throat.

"Grab his wallet, and I want that watch too!" Hiram barked. His hot breath seared Adam's nose with the rank odors of black coffee and unbrushed teeth. He had both hands on Adam's shoulders, keeping him firmly pressed against the wall. Adam's feet were not touching the floor. Horace kept the knife at Adam's throat while he slipped his left hand into Adam's back pocket and took his wallet. He put the wallet into the front pocket of his pants and then he ripped Adam's shirt open, looking for the crucifix pendant. It was not around Adam's neck.

"He's not wearing it!" yelled Horace, obviously surprised. "Where's the necklace? Where's the necklace?" The knife in his right hand started to shake and quiver as the man's emotions started to get the better of him.

"Check his pockets. It's got to be on him," Hiram said.

"It's not here! It's not here!!" Horace protested as he went through Adam's pants pockets. The shaking knife moved closer and closer to Adam's throat.

Hiram released his grip on Adam's shoulders and Adam dropped. Before Adam's feet hit the ground, Hiram punched him in the side of the head. The boulder- sized fist connected squarely on Adam's temple and applied enough pressure to render him unconscious.

The two muggers fled hurriedly out through the front door, leaving it standing wide open. Adam's unconscious body was left lying on the floor in front of it. The flopping of plastic against wooden flooring broke the silence as Adam's phone vibrated next to him. The screen lit up with Adam's caller ID, revealing the call was coming from Uncle Pete.

Chapter 15.

The next morning Adam and Uncle Pete were seated in a red vinyl booth inside the twenty-four-hour diner. The diner had black and white checkered floors with the walls decorated in framed, black and white photographs of early trains and train stations. The booth they were seated in was midway down a long aisle of windows. The two men talked over coffee and half-eaten breakfast platters. Adam's face bore the bruises from the beating he received the night before but reflected no major injuries. In between bites, Pete looked up at Adam, scanning his injuries.

"That's quite a bump on your head," he said, concerned. "Are you sure you don't need to go to the E.R.?"

"I'm sure. I just can't figure out what they were

after," Adam responded.

Pete gave Adam a curious look. "What do you mean? You walked in on two men who were in the process of robbing your house. Thank God you're still alive."

Adam was trying to make sense of the attack. He continued speaking his mind to Pete. "That's the thing. They weren't robbing the house. They turned over every drawer, emptied every cabinet, tossed every piece of furniture, but they didn't take anything. The only things they took were my wallet and watch. And that was after I walked in on them."

"Are you sure that's all they got? Maybe there's something else, something small that you're overlooking," Pete suggested.

"No. That's what seems so strange," Adam said.

"If they took the time to redecorate your whole house, then they had to have been looking for something. Try to think. What do you think they were after? Maybe one of them said something, or did something that you're not remembering."

"I wish I could be more helpful, but nothing is coming to me. I just know I got roughed up and knocked out in my own home," Adam said before taking a sip of his coffee. Adam sneered at the bitter taste of the old overcooked coffee. He reached for the creamer and poured another splash in his cup as he continued trying to unearth the details of the attack from his memory.

Pete continued to eat his egg-white omelet and patiently watched Adam.

"Wait," Adam said suddenly, as he remembered one specific detail. "One of them was looking for a necklace. It's like they expected me to be wearing one," he said, having forgotten about the necklace he had lent Claire.

Pete perked up, his interest piqued more than usual at the mention of a necklace.

"But I don't wear a necklace," Adam continued, not realizing or considering that the robbers might have been looking for the silver crucifix Henry had given him to keep safe. "So I don't know what that's all about."

"Why would they ask you for a necklace? Seems pretty specific, doesn't it?" Pete questioned.

"Yeah, it does. It makes me think that they were in the wrong place. Maybe they thought they were in someone else's apartment," Adam responded, shrugging off the thought that these robbers would be targeting him for some necklace.

"Well, you don't have to go back there if you don't want to. It's obviously not safe. Stay with me, for a few days at least. Then, when you're able to, you can go back, collect your things, and move out of that place," Pete offered, concerned for the welfare of his nephew.

"Thanks for the offer, Uncle Pete, but the best thing for me to do is clean the place up and not let this disrupt how I live my life," Adam said as he felt his cell phone vibrate in his pocket. He reached into his pocket and removed his phone. The screen had lit up and revealed a text message.

"Work?" Pete asked.

"Sort of. There's a press conference at the hospital today. One of my patients had a pretty amazing recovery. The hospital priest declared it a miracle and now the administration is having this media thing to promote the hospital," Adam said, disinterested.

"That's God's work, Adam. You shouldn't shrug it off so easily. You were His instrument in healing someone. Your persistence in attacking the demons within your patient is worth celebrating. You should-"

"I should go. And if it was a miracle, then it's between God and that little girl. I'll see you this weekend at the museum dedication. Um, I would pay but..." Adam said as he patted his pockets, suggesting his wallet was missing.

"Go. I've got this," Pete said and waved Adam off.

Pete stayed at the table and finished his eggs and coffee as he watched Adam get into his car through the large window half covered by a poster with a picture of pancakes and bacon on it. As Adam drove away, Pete noticed the day runner headlights from a car parked half way in an alley across the street turn on. The car pulled out of the alley and quickly headed in the same direction that Adam had left in.

Chapter 16.

The Claire Martinez miracle was all over the local and national news and it was turning out to be a great personal interest story. The hospital public relations department barely had time to gather the facts from statements made by Father Kellen before they were flooded with calls from news agencies, and news vans with cameras and reporters filling the parking lot. Hope Hospital's administration planned to take advantage of the media coverage and use the attention to try to raise funds for the hospital and a new Children's Cancer and Recovery Wing. Members of the public relations department had set up a podium for microphones on the main steps to the hospital in preparation for the inevitable news conference.

Adam avoided the news reporters and entered the

hospital through the Emergency Room doors. As he stepped into the Emergency Room, Adam noticed Elam Bishlam sitting in a wheelchair, being checked out by his niece Amanda. Adam saw that Mr. Bishlam appeared to have been in a nasty accident, but was in good spirits. Adam turned, and was shocked to find his two cousins, Jordy and Sean, seated in the waiting area.

"Sean? Jordy? You guys all right?" Adam asked.

"It's Mom," Sean answered. "We brought her in late last night. She started to have blurriness in her left eye. They finally got her in a couple hours ago."

"You guys should've called me," Adam said with growing concern. "I would've pulled some strings, got her seen sooner. Do you want me to get an update on where they are with her?"

"We're just waiting on the test results," Jordy said.

"Maybe I can try to speed things up," Adam assured his cousins as he left the waiting room to go check in on his aunt.

Helen had been admitted to a room with a view overlooking the front entrance of the hospital. Adam knocked on the door and slowly peered in. Helen was lying on the hospital bed, with her back and head elevated.

"Aunt Helen, how are you feeling?" Adam asked as he

walked to her bedside.

"Oh Adam, you shouldn't bother yourself," Helen replied. "It's probably nothing, just a bout of blurred vision. I can't seem to get my eyes to focus on anything clearly."

"That doesn't sound like nothing."

"What's with all the commotion outside?" Helen asked, changing the subject. "It looks like a bunch of news vans are gathering in front of the hospital. Is one of those celebrity pop stars going through rehab or something here?"

"No, Aunt Helen, no celebrities. Well, one young gal, who seemed to beat cancer overnight. She's a celebrity to us. That's who the news vans are here to see. It was strange, Aunt Helen. I was in the room. She was dying, and then suddenly her body started working to heal on its own. I've never seen anything like it."

"Sounds like a miracle to me."

"That's what they're calling it. I've actually got to get down there. I'll get a doctor up here with your test results."

Adam gave her a gentle squeeze on her forearm and then left the room. He walked over to the nurses' station and asked that a rush be put on all testing and that any information concerning his aunt be communicated to him.

After speaking with the head nurse for a moment, Adam was called to the administration office. He was late for the press conference.

Adam was not prepared for the blinding lights from the multitude of cameras that flashed in his eyes as he stood behind the podium in front of the hospital's main entrance. Doctor Amal Hammurabi, the chief of the hospital, was giving the speech the public relations department had prepared. Adam stood between Claire Martinez and Father Kellen. To the girl's right were her parents, Isabel and Dave. After Doctor Hammurabi had finished, it was Father Kellen's turn to take to the podium.

Father Kellen spoke passionately of the miracle he had witnessed and ended his speech with a short prayer and moment of silence. Once the moment of silence had completed, Adam was ushered to the bank of microphones. Not really knowing what to say, Adam cleared his throat and thought for a moment. He didn't want to disagree with anything the previous speakers had said, even though he didn't personally believe this to be a case of divine intervention. He wanted to be able to explain what had happened to Claire from a scientific standpoint but couldn't. The hospital could use funding for a new recovery wing, and the priest's rendition of the events weren't exaggerated, he thought to himself. So Adam decided to simply congratulate Claire and her family on their strength through their entire ordeal. Adam ended his speech and took his place back in line. Once he was back at Claire's side, she took his hand and gave it a reassuring squeeze.

Near the front entrance, behind the cluster of press, Adam's cousin, Sean, slowly wheeled Helen out of the hospital through the automated doors. Helen looked back over her shoulder in an attempt to catch a peek at the commotion as Sean wheeled her down the ramp towards a waiting black sedan.

Helen looked directly at Claire as Claire held Adam's hand. A glint of sunlight bounced off Claire's neck, causing Helen to squint. As the beam of light cleared, Helen made out the image of a silver crucifix pendant hanging around Claire's neck. A rush of adrenaline shot into her body as she quickly tried to stop and climb out of the wheelchair. Sean lunged and grabbed his mother as she fell to the side of the wheelchair, almost causing him to run her over at the end of the ramp near the loading zone.

"Mom, what are doing?" Sean gasped.

"Stop. Stop," Helen pleaded.

"Come on, Mom. You could've really hurt yourself. Get

into the car," Sean demanded.

Jordy rushed out of the back of the sedan to Sean's aide and help lift his mother Helen up. The two men book-ended their mother, each hooking an arm underneath one of Helen's, and then assisted her over to the waiting car.

"That girl, you idiots," Helen snarled as her boys placed her into the back of the sedan.

Sean slammed the door shut and folded up the wheelchair. He was tired, his skin felt grimy, and, frankly, he had had all the excitement he cared for, for one day. His remaining priorities consisted of getting his mother home, taking a hot bath and introducing his lips to a whiskey sour, in that particular order. He quickly took the wheelchair to the back of the sedan and placed it into the trunk as Helen continued to shout at Jordy in what he thought was a nonsensical fashion. Sean worked his way back up to the front passenger door and loaded himself into the sedan. The driver slowly drove the car off behind the press gathering.

"Circle back around," Helen fumed.

"Mom, you've had a long day," Sean shot back.

"Now!" Helen screamed, like a toddler who was refused a toy.

Helen's driver, not wishing to lose his job, hit the brakes at Helen's command but a security guard standing on the curb quickly blew a whistle and waved for the sedan to drive on. Helen angrily stared down the security guard as her car drove away from the hospital.

The news vans started up their engines, signaling the end of the press conference as the various reporters gathered up their belongings and headed to their respective vehicles.

Helen struggled to stare out of the back window, hoping for one more look at Claire as her sedan drove towards the exit but the crowd of reporters descending on the loading zone and parking lot was too thick for her to see. Behind the thick wave of reporters, Adam still held Claire's hand in his.

She smiled up at him and said, "Good work, Doc."

Adam chuckled to himself.

"Here. You should have this back," Claire said as she removed the necklace from around her neck.

"You keep it," Adam replied.

"No way, dude," Claire answered. "Something tells me this was meant to be with you."

Claire opened up Adam's hand and placed her hand on top of his. She looked up at him and gave a half smile then said simply, "Doc, remember when you helped paint my hand and press it on the hospital wall? It was my first time here. I was four."

Adam nodded silently, remembering the day with great clarity.

"Thank you for holding my hand every step of the way. It was God's will you were my doctor." She slowly lifted her hand off his to reveal his great-grandfather's necklace in his palm. Adam closed his hand and hugged her.

Claire and her family turned and walked back into the hospital with Father Kellen and Doctor Hammurabi. Claire held her father's hand as he and Doctor Hammurabi discussed the paperwork that needed to be signed before Claire's release while her mother and Father Kellen spoke of the miracle that was her daughter's recovery.

Adam stared down at the silver crucifix pendant that lay in his hand frozen with the realization that this might have been the object the robbers were looking for when they broke into his home and attacked him the night before. But how could they have known about it? Or that he possessed it? Even more so, why would they want a simple silver crucifix? Were there actually people out there who believed it possessed the power to heal? That it contained the tip of one of the Holy Nails stained with the blood of Jesus Christ? His great-grandfather had assured him that no one else was even aware of the secret of the necklace, which Adam still considered a myth. Even after witnessing Claire's miraculous recovery, Adam remained highly skeptical. He tried to put the events out of his mind and attributed his paranoia to the heavy emotional stress he'd been under the past few days.

He closed his fingers around the crucifix and stuffed his fist into his front pant pocket. He released the necklace and pulled his hand out of the pocket; the necklace however must have got entangled in his hand and dropped to the ground as he drew his hand out of his pocket. The necklace would have stayed there if not for the slight clinking sound it made when it hit the concrete at Adam's feet.

Adam looked down and stared at the pendant for a moment. The thought of leaving it there for anyone to find crossed his mind, but then the words of his great-grandfather Henry echoed his thoughts. Adam had promised to take the necklace and keep his ownership of it a secret until one day when he would pass it along to someone who needed it. The idea seemed silly, but he felt it would be wrong not to honor a promise, especially a promise made to Henry. Adam bent down and scooped the necklace off the ground. He put the chain over his head and tucked the pendant under his shirt.

"I can't drop it if it's wrapped around my neck," he

muttered to himself. He walked back into the hospital and noticed the strange feeling of having something around his neck. He wasn't used to it. For a moment he was sure that he would remove it as soon as he got to his desk, but the strange feeling subsided and Adam forgot he was wearing it before he got twenty feet down the hall.

Chapter 17.

A few days had passed since the press conference and Adam was surprised by how many strangers were still walking up to him on the street to congratulate him. They had either read about the miracle at the hospital or seen the coverage on television. The limelight and attention was beginning to make him feel uncomfortable and in need of a reclusive vacation somewhere. He barely saw Rose at work as the hospital chief kept him busy doing photo ops and politicking for foundation grants on behalf of the hospital. He contemplated cancelling his date that evening with Rose and just spending the evening at home with a good movie, but he was obligated to be in attendance at the museum. It was the night the John C. Trever Museum of History was holding a dedication to his great-grandfather, and the dedication to Henry Calhoun was well attended.

News crews from all over covered the event as everyone who was anyone attended. Attendees were greeted at the entrance by museum employees handing out colorful brochures that gave a brief description on Henry's life as an archeologist, included a map of the new wing and photographs of some of the artifacts on display. Catering staff bustled along within the crowd with large silver trays filled with hors d'oeuvres and champagne as people viewed the displays. The smaller items were placed on pedestals, under glass; the larger items were placed behind velvet ropes attached to brass stanchions. All of the rooms and a number of individual items were flanked by security guards. Some of the relics on display were Joseph Kaifa's ossuary, Pontius Pilot's inscription on a building stone that was found at Caesarea Maritima, the ruins of a boat discovered near the shore of the Sea of Galilee, referred to as "The Jesus Boat", James' ossuary, and the skeleton of a crucified man among many others.

In the main hall, Helen sat in a wheelchair, flanked by her two sons, Jordy and Sean. Pete stood at the podium giving a short speech about his grandfather to the black tie crowd. Adam and Rose stood arm in arm off to the side, listening intently. Rose looked stunning in her form fitting, baby-blue cocktail dress and that put Adam at ease, allowing him to feel as if all eyes were on her and not him; so much so that Adam failed to notice the tall gaunt man watching him intently from the crowd.

After Pete's speech, the crowd dispersed to return to viewing the displays. Adam and Rose walked over to Helen to say hello. When Adam bent down to give Helen a hug, Rose saw that Helen grabbed at his neck with her right hand, and began petting and sweeping her hand from shoulder to shoulder. Adam asked if she was all right. Helen assured him that she was, and stated that she was just straightening Adam's collar then she unbuttoned the top button of his shirt and told him to relax. Rose found this behavior pretty odd, and her face evidently showed it because as she and Adam walked away, Adam leaned closer to her and whispered, "My aunt is getting a bit eccentric."

"You think?" Rose replied. "I do agree with her on the top button thing though... you look better with it undone."

"You don't think the chest hair is too much...a little too *Miami Vice*." Adam smiled and walked with a little more swagger than normal.

"Sign of a strong man. So long as you don't start wearing any gold chains with a clock or something weird around your neck, the look works for me."

"I can assure you I don't wear necklaces," Adam said.

The events that had occurred during the week prior, from Aunt Helen's angry outburst about the missing necklace to the robbery that occurred at Adam's apartment, made Adam extremely mindful not to reveal or even discuss the necklace with the silver crucifix pendant that Henry had given him. This policy appeared to be working out as things had been pretty uneventful in regards to the necklace lately. He was happy to report that he had not experienced any threats, break-ins or miracles since the press conference and even considered himself silly for the split second he thought the necklace might actually possess a major Christian relic. But just to be extra cautious around his family during the museum dedication and dinner, Adam made sure to keep the necklace safely hidden in a pouch in his front pant pocket.

As they approached the exhibit and the crowd, Adam slowed his pace. Rose extended her hand for Adam to take. He accepted it and Rose then took the lead and pulled Adam through the exhibit like an excited schoolgirl on a field trip. During their walk through the exhibit, Adam found himself quite impressed by Rose and how knowledgeable she was about the artifacts on display. She did have to read from the brochure about some of the lesser known items, but it seemed that she was not just Henry's doctor but also a fan of his work. At the end of the first corridor was the Iron Crown exhibit, which was flanked by two security guards and safely set behind a bullet-proof casing.

"The Iron Crown of Lombardy!" Rose blurted excitedly. "It's called the Iron Crown because of a narrow band of iron within it that is said to have been beaten out of one of the nails from Christ's crucifixion."

"Really?" Adam asked. "What else do you know about it?"

"Well, according to legend," Rose began, "the nail was given to Emperor Constantine by his mother, St. Helena, who had discovered the cross. Now, supposedly, she cast one of the nails into the sea to calm a storm. Another was fitted to the head of a statue of the emperor, another one was incorporated into Constantine's helmet, and the fourth one was molded into a bit for his horse. Some say that several fragments of one of the nails were sent off to dignitaries as objects of diplomacy. One of the recipients of such a gift was Princess Theodelinda, who used her nail as part of her crown. The crown was later used in Charlemagne's coronation as King of the Lombards. Most accounts of the initiations of Kings of the Lombards say that the kings also took in hand a Holy Lance."

"Wow!" Adam said, obviously impressed by Rose's knowledge. "You seem to really know your crowns."

"I minored in art history. I actually wrote a thesis paper on religious art and artifacts and their impact on our social development. I would have loved to have known your great-grandfather when I was writing that paper. It would have saved me hours in the library."

"Want some insider knowledge?" Adam asked.

"I'd love some," Rose said as she stepped closer to Adam.

"That crown is a fake," Adam whispered. "Well, not the crown, but the story about the nail. I have it on good authority that the nail was not used in this crown."

"Really?" Rose's curiosity was piqued. "Well then, mister smarty pants, where is the nail?"

Rose flirtatiously leaned in toward Adam, either to get a kiss or to have Adam whisper the secret into her ear. She passed his lips and brushed her cheek against his. Adam couldn't help but notice her perfume, a light lavender, and baby powder wafting into his nostrils as she flicked her hair back, revealing her ear centimeters away from his mouth. Just as Adam opened his lips to speak, unsure of whether to reveal the secret that was tucked away in his pocket or tell her another one of Henry's stories, a voice came from behind him.

"It's in the Vatican."

Adam turned, startled and saw a tall gaunt grey-haired man, looking to be in his early sixties and dressed in all black.

"Excuse me?" Rose asked, insinuating to the man that he was interrupting a private conversation.

"The nail is protected in the Vatican," the man said. "My name is Father Claudio. I've been sent to investigate the miracle that was said to have occurred at the hospital. I would like to interview you, Dr. Calhoun, regarding your account of the incident. I assure you, the Vatican is approaching this incident very cautiously, but whenever something like this garners so much attention, well, with the internet and all, we do have to act quickly."

"Now?" Adam asked. He was clearly taken off guard and began to sweat.

"If you have a few moments?" Father Claudio asked. "We could talk briefly in private outside on one of the balconies if you prefer."

Rose looked around to see if anyone else in the room was paying any attention to the conversation the two men were having, and noticed Helen watching them suspiciously from a distance.

"Can it wait?" Rose asked. "We have dinner reservations on the roof."

"Of course," Father Claudio conceded. "Perhaps I could come by your home, Dr. Calhoun?"

"The hospital would be better," Adam said. "Anytime during the week. My shift usually ends around seven."

"Thank you," Father Claudio said. "Peace be with you both. Enjoy your dinner."

***

Helen stared as the priest walked away from the couple and Adam and Rose headed toward the elevator. Pete walked up behind Helen's wheelchair.

"What is the matter with you?" Pete asked. "You've got that I'm-plotting-something-rotten look on your face again."

"Last week at the hospital," Helen replied, "there was a girl they were interviewing."

"Yes, Adam's miracle patient," Pete said. "She's been all over the news."

"I was at the hospital that day, and I could've sworn she had Gramps' necklace."

"Helen, really?" Pete asked, fed up with Helen's obsessive conspiracy-filled crusade to find Henry's necklace. "That's a bit farfetched, even for you."

"I'm being serious. I saw her wearing something when she was standing with Adam when I was leaving the hospital. I can't be positive, but I have this gut feeling it was the necklace, Pete. I just know it."

"You SAW her, in your condition? You, who told me

you can barely see your television remote? Let it go, Helen. The necklace is lost and that's all there is to it. This isn't a treasure hunt. Stop obsessing. Paranoia is going to take hold of you and then you'll find yourself in an insane asylum. Let's go up and get something to eat." Pete pushed Helen's wheelchair to the elevator and pressed the button for the top floor restaurant, the OSIRIS.

Egyptian God of the Dead

***

The posh OSIRIS restaurant resided on the rooftop of The John C. Trever Museum of History and was elegantly decorated for the private party of exclusive VIPS and family members there to celebrate the work of the late Henry Calhoun. The dining room area shone like an ice castle with frosted glass dining tables, each topped with a single crystal votive containing a deep purple candle. The tables were surrounded by elegant blue leather seats and faux crystal columns that reflected deep blue and green LED lights shooting up towards the heavens. Servers wearing crisp white shirts, black aprons and black pants moved meticulously amongst the tables, serving the pre-planned menu.

Adam sat across from Rose at a table for two overlooking the city skyline. He was finally starting to decompress, which, ironically, was making for a rather poor dinner date for Rose. He was quietly, sliding several maple-glazed carrots to and fro on his plate that contained a partially eaten tilapia fillet and white cheddar mashed potatoes covered in a white cream sauce. The grief at Henry's death, which Adam had been fighting off, was finally starting to creep in. He slid a carrot into a mound of mash potatoes and thought of the museum exhibit and his great-grandfather's life's work.

Rose watched him in silence, searching for a clear opportunity to grab his attention without seeming desperate for conversation. "The carrots sure are tricky to handle," she said.

Adam stopped playing plate hockey with his food just long enough to glance up at Rose with a somewhat embarrassed expression on his face. "I'm sorry. I used to do this as a kid when I had a lot on my mind."

"Anything you want to talk about? I have a great pair of ears. They're a little oversized for my head, but all the better to hear you with." Rose chuckled slightly and paused for a moment, awaiting his response.

Adam took in a deep breath and jutted out his bottom teeth, biting up on his top lip. He remained silent but his body language was clearly showing signs of a man dealing with tremendous anxiety.

"Is the robbery still bothering you?" Rose asked

cautiously.

Adam tilted his head side to side in a "so-so" motion.

"Did the police get any leads?"

"No. I don't think so. I haven't heard anything. Time sure does fly, doesn't it? Feels like my Papa Henry was just here an hour ago. I wanted to pick up my cell phone and call him to get down here and take a bow." Adam released a smile from ear to ear at Rose as he quickly shifted emotional gears. "Did you enjoy the exhibit?"

"I did. It's amazing to think of all the things Henry must have seen in his life. He must have shared some amazing stories with you," Rose said.

"He had his moments for sure but he loved to talk about charity. Helping the children's hospital or visiting orphanages. He was always stressing the importance of making people feel like they belonged, had purpose, especially kids. When I went to live with him after my mother died, he was already in his eighties. He was mainly focused on his charities."

"Come on. He must have had some stories to tell — cursed diamonds or mysterious origins," Rose said with a playful smirk.

"Okay, there was one story he was fond of telling. It was about a particular dig in Turkey in the 1920s in Colossae."

"Colossae? Are you referring to the ancient city on the Lycus? Adam, Colossae has never been excavated."

"Not officially. However, Henry and an associate went alone on a secret mission to locate part of a large stone that had been scarred by a lightning strike. According to the story, pagans had diverted the stream of a river to flow against the sanctuary of St. Michael in order to destroy it."

"You're referring to the miracle of the archangel Michael?"

"Yes. As the water was eroding the walls and foundation of the sanctuary away, many of the poor and sick housed inside were in danger of being swept into the river or crushed under the thick walls of the sanctuary as it fell. But before the walls gave way, Michael the archangel appeared and split a huge stone by lightning, protecting the sanctuary by diverting the flow away from the church thus sanctifying forever the waters that come from the gorge. Henry and his assistant had to disguise themselves as sheep herders while they tunneled to the site of the sanctuary and remove a chipped part of the scarred stone. Once the stone fragment was in their possession, their only goal was to avoid being killed."

Rose leaned forward in her seat, captivated by the story and hungry to hear more. Adam took a sip of water and continued the story.

"They were in the middle of the Greco-Turkish War and they had somehow become part of the Battle of Kütahya–Eskişehir. The Greek Army had managed to break through Turkish resistance and occupied the towns of Kara Hisâr Sahib, Kütahya and Eskişehir, together with their inter-connecting rail lines. Papa and his associate were planning on using one of the rail lines to get the stone out of Turkey. The Turks were being defeated, so, somehow, Papa helped the Turks avoid encirclement and together they made a strategic retreat to the east side of the Sakarya River. That gave the Turkish army adequate time to organize their defenses, and Henry and his associate an opportunity to deliver the stone to the Vatican."

Rose glanced to her left, and noticed Adam's aunt was seated at a table approximately forty feet away from them with Pete and the curator of the museum. Pete and the curator were speaking casually as Helen did her best Nancy Drew impression in a sad attempt to spy on Adam and Rose through a pair of gold-rimmed opera binoculars.

"Your Aunt Helen sure does take an interest in you, that's for sure."

"What is she doing now?" Adam sighed.

"Oh, just staring at us through a pair of opera

116

glasses."

Rose waved at Helen politely. Helen fumbled to place the binoculars onto the glass table after noticing Rose was onto her.

"I think she missed her calling in life." Rose laughed.

"I'm sure the CIA could use an unassuming master spy," Adam volleyed back.

"I was thinking she would have made a great boarding school Mother Superior. I had my share growing up."

"Boarding school, huh? Ouch. Broken rulers over the knuckles and all that?"

"For some." Rose laughed. "But I was a model citizen. I actually really enjoyed boarding school. It was like I had dozens of sisters overnight."

"Do you have any brothers or sisters?"

"Nope. Only child, and my parents are missionaries so I rarely saw them growing up. They were always off in some remote place with no technology, so the nuns in boarding school felt like great company for me."

Adam raised his glass in a toast. "Well, here's to present great company."

Rose raised her glass, clinking it against his as she locked eyes with Adam in a loving gaze.

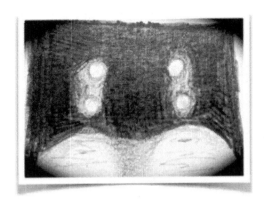

Chapter 18.

Later that night, Adam drove his car down a quiet tree-lined street and parked in front of the duplex apartment building that Rose had been calling home for several years.

"Thank you for the great evening," Rose said with her hands clasped onto the handbag in her lap. "Would you like to come inside for a night cap?"

"I would love to," Adam said, "but I really have to be getting home." The photo of Tara beside his bed called to his thoughts.

"OK," Rose said. She pulled on the door handle to let herself out, but the door was locked.

"Here, let me," Adam said quickly as he got out of the car, ran around to the passenger side, and opened Rose's door for her.

"Thank you," Rose whispered in Adam's ear as she kissed him on the cheek, her left hand lightly touching his chest. Then she walked to her apartment.

Adam stood beside his car and watched Rose enter her home. Once he was satisfied that she was safely inside, Adam drove away. As he pulled away from the curb to head down the street, the headlights from a car parked half a block behind him came on. The car pulled out and began to follow him at a steady pace.

Adam listened to his favorite jazz station as he negotiated the traffic signals and other cars on the road. Each time he checked his rear view mirror, he noticed the same pair of double headlights from an unfamiliar car behind him. Alarmed, Adam decided to circle around that area of town a couple of times to see if the car would head off in a different direction. The car continued to follow him, matching his maneuvers, move for move. In a panic, Adam activated the speaker phone function on his cell phone and called his Uncle Pete.

"Someone's following me!" Adam said as soon as Pete picked up his phone.

"Are you sure?" Pete asked. "Maybe they're just going the same way."

"I've driven in two circles and the car is still behind me. I'm not sure what I should do."

"Drive to my house. If they are still behind you when you pull up the drive, honk your horn twice and stay in your car until I come out to get you."

Adam considered his uncle's advice as he turned onto Amber Way and headed toward Pete's house. Then Adam considered another approach. He quickly pulled his car over to the shoulder. The car that had been following him skidded past and erratically pulled over onto the shoulder in front of Adam's car.

The driver, wearing dark clothing, stepped out of the dark sedan. Adam slammed the gas pedal of his car hard to the floor. The rubber from his tires smoked and peeled as he sped past the other driver. Adam shot a look out his passenger window and tried to get a look at the other man. All he saw was a dark figure, a black suit and what appeared to be the white rectangle of a priest's collar. Adam kept his foot heavy on the gas pedal all the way to Pete's house.

Twenty minutes later, Adam found himself in the safety of Pete's estate, pacing back and forth in the foyer of the grand mansion as he framed together the details of the chase in his mind. His hand was clasped to his forehead, rubbing his temples with his thumb on one side and forefinger on the other. Paranoia and fear had started to grip Adam again. Tonight's events could not simply be chalked up to another coincidence. Adam knew for sure that he was a target now but the reason as to why remained a mystery.

Was the robbery of his apartment somehow tied to the man who was following him tonight? The robbers demanded he give them his necklace. Did they somehow know about the story behind the gift he'd received from Henry on his death bed? Henry was adamant that no one else knew about its significance, and Adam still felt he had every reason to believe this. After all, his great-grandfather lived to be 119 years old and if someone wanted it badly enough, why not go after Henry while he was still alive? Even so, Adam's thoughts continued racing through his mind, unable to put the pieces of the puzzle together as his belief system fought off other possibilities like a heavily armed immune system chasing down a cold.

What if the stories were true? No, that's absurd, Adam thought, as his mind continued the philosophical fight with itself. A spiritual war had not raged in his head regarding the truth or absence of God this much since Tara passed away. If there were people who believe the necklace that rested in his pocket was some major religious artifact, then being chased by a priest might not be so crazy. There was only one way Adam would get to

121

the truth, and that would be to risk opening himself up to the possibility of much more. He had to confide in someone. The burden was beginning to feel intolerable. Why not confide in the next closest person to a father figure Adam had left? He took a deep breath, stopped pacing, and stared Uncle Pete directly in the eyes as he prepared to spill the beans about everything, including the necklace.

"This is going to sound stupid, I know, but it was a priest who was chasing me."

"A priest?" Pete asked, an incredulous look on his face. "Those guys who broke into your house hit you pretty hard on the head, didn't they?"

"Or someone dressed as a priest. I know it sounds ridiculous," Adam said candidly.

"Why would a priest, or someone posing as a priest, want to run you off the road?"

Adam looked down, put his hand in his pocket, and felt the mass of the pendant under his fingers. He was torn between keeping the promise he'd made to his great-grandfather, and telling Pete every morsel. Henry's weighty words, "Do not tell anyone," rang in his ears like an old Irish bell tower calling the congregation to Sunday service. But Adam was alone in this and as much as his hubris tried to convince himself the recent events were

122

coincidental, he just couldn't stop the strong feeling that everything was connected to his great-grandfather's passing, the necklace, or both. Before he could censor his vocal cords and stomach the secret once more, his mouth vomited every letter of the alphabet in relaying detail by detail the sequence of events he had experienced from Henry handing him the necklace through tonight.

After what seemed like hours of Pete standing in silence listening to Adam's tale of inheritance, robbery, miraculous healing and his recent relationship with Rose, he walked dumbfounded over to Adam and wrapped his arms around the distraught and emotionally exhausted young man.

"So what are you going to do now?" Pete asked.

"Keep going how I'm going until I can figure this thing out."

"And the necklace?"

Adam removed his hand from his pocket, having decided to keep the necklace's location a secret. "I made a promise to Papa Henry and I am keeping that promise."

"Your Aunt Helen would flip out if she knew you had it. She already thinks everyone from the funeral home to that pretty doctor you're dating, Rose, stole it."

"Papa gave it to me, not Helen. Not anyone else. I am sure he did so for a reason. This is none of her business, and I am trusting that you will keep this between us, Uncle Pete."

"I gave you my word. But still, your aunt, she sees things differently than the rest of us when it comes to Gramps. You could always give me the necklace and I could tell Helen that they found it at the funeral home under the embalming table or somewhere. She can lock it away in the family lockbox. No one will know. You don't need this burden in your life."

"If people are really after the necklace, what's going to prevent them from still thinking I have it? I'll take my chances and hold on to it. At least I have some semblance of control that way."

"Then I want you to move into my house. Over eight thousand square feet is more than one man should ever endure alone. You'll be good company for me and I can hire some security to stay on the property."

"I appreciate that but I don't want any changes."

"I have to insist on this, Adam."

"I can handle my own safety, Uncle Pete. Papa Henry lived to be 119 years old with this necklace, and no one was out to get him in the end."

"Now is not a time to act invincible. Your great-grandpa wasn't always the man you idolized. He had secrets. Lots of them. Danger comes in all forms, Adam."

"What kind of secrets?" Adam asked.

"Who can say for sure if what he used to tell us was true or what parts were just some fantasy tale told to amuse us as children. I just remember my mom talking about how she had found out that Gramps used to work for the Vatican when he was younger and there was a falling out."

"Did she say what caused the falling out?"

"No. Look, Adam, no one knows who else Gramps told over the years about that necklace. Just be careful. Regardless of whether or not what he said is true, belief is a strong motivator— it drives people to do good deeds but can push people to do evil as well. That makes that little iron relic you have from him very dangerous in my book."

"If what Gramps said is true, then God should intervene, right?" Adam said with a hint of cynical hope.

"Let me tell you a bedtime story Gramps used to tell your mom, Aunt Helen and me when we were little. There once was a man named Peter Bartholomew. He was a French soldier who was part of the First Crusade. During the Siege of Antioch, Peter claimed that Saint Andrew appeared to him and, through visions, took him inside Antioch to the Church of St. Peter and showed him where the relic of the Holy Lance could be found. Saint Andrew then instructed Peter to tell the Crusade leaders and to

125

give the Lance to Raymond of St. Gilles when it was found. Peter did not immediately inform Raymond or the other leaders and was visited four more times. Peter began to lose his sight in February of 1098. He believed Saint Andrew was punishing him. The Crusaders captured Antioch. Peter and Raymond began excavating the floor of the church. Peter discovered the Lance and was visited once more by Saint Andrew that night, who told him to establish a feast day in honor of the discovery. Many people believed that Peter was a charlatan and that he had brought a piece of iron with him to stage a false find. Word of the supposed false claim spread, and Peter's reputation was tarnished. In 1099 on April 8th, Peter went through an ordeal by fire by his own choice in an attempt to prove himself. He was severely burned in the process, although he claimed he was uninjured because Christ had appeared to him in the fire. In any case, he died."

Adam considered the story for a moment. He couldn't make a connection between his being followed and the story of Peter Bartholomew. "I'm not following, Uncle Pete."

"The moral of the story is the Lord does not intervene. He only provides us with guidance. The choice of whether to step into the fire or walk away from it is ultimately up to us. Adam, if you are going to hang onto that old iron relic, please be extremely cautious. You don't know what you might be getting yourself into. I doubt you are the only person Gramps told about it." Pete yawned and looked at the clock on the wall. "I'm tired, and I'm ready for bed. You should stay here tonight. It's safe here. Sleep in the first guest room at the top of the stairs. We can talk more in the morning."

Pete patted Adam on the upper arm and then walked up the great staircase and went to his room. Adam considered his uncle's proposal and realized that he would not be able to sleep in Pete's guest room. He felt the need to get to his own home and to the photo of Tara. He also had an important appointment with Eli the following evening that he couldn't miss and needed to be rested up for. He quietly left Pete's house and drove home, checking his rear view mirror every few seconds for followers. There were none. As Adam drove, he couldn't help but ponder the story of Peter Bartholomew and what connections there were between him and Henry, if any.

Chapter 19.

It was a standing-room only crowd at the "Second Coming" event. Five hundred and eighty hopeful parishioners, with ailments ranging from mild allergies to paraplegics in wheelchairs, filled the rental hall that had been converted into a makeshift church for the event. Each one had come to the event hoping to be chosen for a healing by Pastor Faith. The seating area was arranged into two main areas, with walking aisles on each side and one down the middle. A raised white- carpeted platform with a small mahogany table flanked by two red velvet-upholstered high-backed chairs with mahogany legs and a microphone stand served as the focal point of the room. On the small mahogany table stood a clear glass of water and the well-worn Bible that Pastor Faith used during the service. On the first of the three steps up to the platform stood Pastor Faith, a microphone in his right hand, and his left on the forehead of a twenty-year-old girl named Emily who had come to the event hoping to get her cystic acne cleared up.

Pastor Faith, dressed in an all-white suit, squeezed the young girl's forehead slightly as he prayed over her and asked the crowd to hold their hands out in faith that the healing power of Jesus come through them and cure this young girl's acne and end her social problem. After a moment of silence, Pastor Faith released the girl, who immediately fell in a faint. Two men, ushers who were dressed in black suits and standing at her side during the healing, caught the young girl and dragged her off to the side of the room where a soft light blue shag carpet had been laid and six other unconscious people lay napping. The crowd erupted in applause and screams of 'Praise Jesus' filled the hall.

Pastor Faith raised the microphone to his mouth and took a couple of measured deep breaths to regain his strength. "Ladies and gentlemen," Pastor Faith said, "the power that flows through me will heal that young woman's horrible debilitating acne in time. We must have faith that everything happens in its own time. And speaking of time, I must take a short break while the usher ministries pass around the collection baskets to receive your offerings." Pastor Faith put the microphone back on its stand on the raised platform and walked to the back of the platform and through a door that led to his dressing room.

The dressing room was set up simply with a large mirrored dressing table made of redwood. There was a small white vase holding a single red rose and a hairbrush on the table top. In front of the table was a matching redwood chair with a red velvet cushion. Pastor Faith sat in the chair and faced the mirrored table. He plucked the rose from its vase and held it to his nose, inhaling its aroma and then returned it to its vase. He took the brush and considered pulling it through his perfectly quaffed red hair, but decided the touch up was unnecessary and put the brush down. Next, he opened the top right drawer and took out his cell phone, expecting to have a voicemail message. The clock on the cell phone changed from 8:03 to 8:04. The cell phone vibrated in his hand, signaling an incoming call.

"You're late," Pastor Faith hissed as he answered the call. "Do you have the necklace?"

"Not yet, boss," Hiram hesitantly replied.

"Then what are you doing wasting my time calling me with a failed report?" Pastor Faith yelled into the phone. "You two buffoons have one job to do! One job! Get me *easy to make fun of*

that necklace!" Pastor Faith recovered his composure and with his beaming Southern charm and accent back in place, said, "The Second Coming is upon us, you idiot. He will reveal himself this year. And he has asked me for the cross on that necklace. We cannot fail him."

"We dug up the dead guy's grave," Hiram whined, "and checked the casket. We ransacked the doctor's house and practically beat the guy to death. He doesn't have it."

"He does have it!" Pastor Faith shrieked, losing his composure again. "He healed that girl in the hospital! He's just hidden it somewhere." Pastor Faith paused and thought for a moment. "You have to get him to use it."

"How do we do that?"

"Hurt someone he cares about."

"He has been seeing a real cute little lady lately."

"Perfect! Kidnap his new love interest, and tell him that you'll kill her unless he brings you the necklace."

"What if he doesn't bring it?"

"Then kill her and find someone he does care about enough to save!"

Pastor Faith ended the call and dropped the cell phone back into the drawer. He took up the hair brush and ran it through his hair to regain his composure. He examined his appearance, checking every line on his face to make sure the kindness of the faith healer that everyone knew and loved was shining through.

"The Second Coming is upon us," Pastor Faith said to his own reflection. "He will reveal himself. I must not fail him now."

Know who the bad boss

Chapter 20.

souce   church

Eli sat in the passenger seat of Adam's Honda, picking at his nails as Adam drove the car through the city streets towards All Souls Catholic Church. The roads were relatively quiet for a weekday night. The radio was off in the car as Adam was busy inquiring about Eli's health plan.

"Your nurse tells me that you've gotten more agreeable. That doesn't sound like you. You've also lost some weight. Are you eating OK?" Adam said, concerned.

"I haven't been very hungry lately. I'm not throwing up or anything, just not hungry. I'm also tired of arguing with 'Nurse Ratchet'. Maybe she's growing on me. Speaking of which, you still haven't answered my question. Have you broken down and gone out on a date yet?" Eli retorted.

"What about headaches?" Adam continued, side-stepping Eli's question.

"Other than the ones I get from worrying about you and your wasted love life, no."

"I want you to have your doctor schedule an ultrasound for you. I want them to get a look at your liver and spleen, and get some more blood work done."

"Stop acting like a doctor!" Eli snapped.

"Sorry, occupational hazard."

"Yea, well, you're not my doctor. Just act like my friend. You know, that dopey guy from high school who used to just talk to me, dude to dude."

"We are talking."

"No, you're instructing. Are you acting like this because we're going to an End of Life seminar? If you can't handle it, then just drop me off and I will catch a cab home."

"I can handle it."

"Then stop avoiding the real conversation, which is how are you, not me, you, doing? You look like you haven't slept in weeks. You're hiding something, or someone." Eli got an idea and a gleam in his eye. "Who is she?"

"Who is who?" Adam asked.

"Are you dating one of your patients? You sick, sick

man! Or worse, you're dating Nurse Terry aren't you! Ew!" Eli joked, trying to pry the news out of Adam. "I can keep going all night at this guessing game."

"Okay, okay! You're relentless, you know that? Yes, I went on a date—dates." Adam blushed like a thirteen-year-old who'd just been kissed.

"Oooh. Plural, as in dates equals dating this person?"

"Yes. And no, she's not a patient. She's a doctor. She was my Papa Henry's doctor."

"Uh, don't tell me she's 106 years old and likes knitting yarn cats or something."

"Her name is Rose. She's a few years younger than me, pretty, smart. Look, we just started dating. What more do you want me to say, Inspector? I feel good around her."

"You should be a lot happier than this. You've met somebody worth getting to know! You should be ecstatic, all blushing and gushing and crap. It's not me, is it? I've already told you, I've accepted what's coming. Don't feel bad for me."

"You're right, I should be ecstatic. Rose is a wonderful woman. I just .... It's not you, E.J. I am a little concerned about your loss of appetite, but... it's just that so much weird stuff has been happening. Papa Henry's funeral, the press conference at the hospital, reporters everywhere, getting mugged in my own home, the museum dedication, Aunt Helen is going blind, and just last night, I'm pretty sure that a priest tried to follow me home. It's all a bit too much for me to handle right now."

"God doesn't give us more that we can handle, Adam. He gives us what we need to grow," Eli stated confidently.

"All of this doesn't seem strange to you?"

"You're right—it is odd that you are finally dating someone," Eli teased.

"I'm serious, man."

"When people are going through moments of trauma or grief, sometimes all they see is the negative that's happening in their lives; heck, even the positive stuff can start to look negative."

Adam turned down an oak-lined street, passing a series of single-story homes. The car's headlights illuminated the corner of the street ahead, which was encompassed by All Souls Catholic Church. He drove his car passed the smooth plaster and brick facade of the church and turned into the parking lot.

The parking lot contained about a dozen or so vehicles. Several people, ranging in ages and levels of health, from a silver-haired octogenarian weighing in at about eighty pounds with two men on either side of her helping her walk to a middle-aged man in an electric wheelchair, were filing into the church building. Adam and Eli followed the crowd to the entrance to the church.

The attendees of the End of Life seminar were greeted at the door by a short elderly woman with dyed pink hair and a slight hunch that prevented her from looking up. Her name was Janet Thorntide and she was the coordinating director of church events, and had been for at least thirty years. As Adam and Eli entered, she smiled a delicate closed-lipped smile that lit up her wrinkled face and handed Eli a binder. Adam nodded in thanks and continued to follow Eli through the doors to the church and down the aisle through the ocean of wooden pews stained a light puritan pine color. The walls were lined with plaster engravings representing the Stations of the Cross. Mixed in between the engravings at equal distances were a series of stained glassed windows portraying various saints such as St. Thomas Aquinas, St. Francis of Assisi, St. Peter, St. Paul, St. Dominic and St. Theresa of Avila, to name a few.

Adam recalled an argument his great-grandfather Henry had once had with a non-Catholic friend and colleague, who accused Henry of having a faith that worshiped saints. Henry was quick to school his colleague of this misconception, informing the man that Catholics do not worship saints, but pray in communion with the saints. The stained-glass images reminded Adam of the respect, honor and veneration his papa had towards the saints. Henry would often tell the young Adam with a bright smile, "There's nothing wrong with having a few more friends in heaven petitioning God on our behalf."

Adam spotted a young woman in her early twenties kneeling in prayer off in the side sanctuary. She was kneeling before the glow of flickering candles placed row upon row resting on a votive candle rack used for occasions such as memorializing the departed. Adam stopped in his tracks, Tara weighing heavily on his mind as he watched the young lady light a single candle. The grief was still very much alive deep within the hidden chambers of Adam's heart where he had a habit of locking away his grief and despair. The locker contained the memories of his mother, Tara, his great-grandfather Henry and soon, he thought, his best friend Eli.

"Adam," Eli called to his best friend, snapping Adam out of his momentary daze. Eli waved Adam towards him. The two men continued down the aisle and took seats in the pew that was second from the front row, directly in front of the podium. Once all of those in attendance had settled down in the first few rows of the church, Janet took her position at the podium to begin the seminar.

"Welcome to All Soul's Catholic Church. I would like

to introduce Monsignor McCoy, who will be leading this evening's seminar," she said. She bent her left arm and hand out slightly as she turned to invite Monsignor McCoy, a middle-aged, round-faced and somewhat squatty man with a very kind disposition, to the podium.

"Thank you, Ms. Thorntide," Monsignor McCoy said with a smile, the bass of his voice echoing like a warm tidal wave throughout the church. "I would like to start off the evening with a prayer of health and thanks."

The various attendees blessed themselves and lowered their heads in one robotic but genuine and devotional fashion. Adam joined suit as a sign of respect and the monsignor continued his prayer of welcome. As the prayer went on, Adam's mind began to pick up where it had left off at the remembrance candle. He saw his friend, Eli, deep in prayer from the corner of his eye. All of these folks were gathered in support of one another and to make plans for the reality of life; the reality that one day all living things will die. Only, the atmosphere of this collective seemed to be one of ease and a sense of calm and community. Adam arrogantly felt as if he may be the only one in the place who felt angry at the thought of losing their loved one. He grew increasingly anxious as sweat began to pool in his underarms. His neck felt hot and itchy as if he had a wool shirt buttoned around and

139

starched to his neck. His fast-paced life and the strains of recent events hadn't given him a moment of downtime to reflect on and settle into the other happenings in his life. And here, under the vaulted ceilings of the church, time slowed down and reflection was thrust upon him.

After the prayer, Monsignor McCoy guided all of those in attendance through the carefully laid out binder they'd been given. The binder was divided into sections and detailed all the aspects one might need to cover when it came to end-of-life planning, ranging from estate planning, wills, legal issues regarding power of attorneys, health directives to sacramental rites and the various church-approved options for funeral readings and music selections, which Janet read through for all in attendance. Each section was laid out in an easy, step-by- step, fill-in-the-blanks guide.

Janet assisted the monsignor as they introduced expert guests specializing in each field such as an attorney to speak on legal subjects and a hospital delegate to speak on end-of-life health directives from a medical standpoint.

Eli turned to Adam as the seminar neared completion and gently nudged his shoulder. "You're a true pal," he said with a nod. "Thank you."

Chapter 21.

The hospital walkways still buzzed from time to time with the excitement from the recent miracle, but things were finally slowly getting back to normal. A few stray photographers sat in the main lobby waiting room, which was as far as the hospital security staff would allow them to go. Each one was hoping to get a shot of the famous doctor Adam Calhoun and sell the photo to a supermarket rag.

Adam started his hospital rounds as usual, by checking in with the nursing staff to receive updates on each of his patients. Adam was a very hands-on oncologist, and the hospital nursing staff respected him highly. He wanted to know everything about his patient's inpatient experience. During these morning meetings, Adam would often ask the nursing staff about the patient's general mood, what they ate during meal time, if they'd had visitors, and if they'd had any special requests.

After his morning updates, Adam spent four hours visiting the patients, and not all of them were his own. Often if another oncologist was busy, they would ask Adam to perform what they called surveillance visits to asymptomatic patients with negative scans. Adam performed all of these visits with professionalism, and a friendliness that can only be compared to the kind one might find on their grandmother's front porch swing on a lazy summer evening. After the visits, Adam had lunch in the cafeteria, and then he spent some time in the afternoon keeping up with his office responsibilities. There were no surgeries scheduled for the day so Adam headed to the cafeteria to pick up his dinner.

Adam walked slowly down the long maze of corridors through the hospital that separated the oncology department and the cafeteria. Half way along, Adam passed by the large double doorway that led to the main lobby; three photographers quickly jumped to their feet to snap pictures of Adam walking by.

Adam turned the corner and ignored the sign that read CAFETERIA CLOSED. He walked up to the counter where Lydia sat reading her magazine. Father Claudio, who was seated at a table for two in the corner of the cafeteria, had seen Adam enter the cafeteria, and he quickly got out of his seat and joined him at the counter. Adam didn't notice Father Claudio until he was right beside him. Startled by his sudden appearance, Adam jumped and let out a little yelp.

"Dr. Calhoun," Father Claudio said. "Sorry I startled you. You asked me to stop by after your shift for our interview. I saw the photographers in the lobby so I asked the receptionist where the best place to meet you would be, and she suggested your office. But I didn't want to disturb your work so I thought I would wait for you here."

"Right," Adam said, collecting his nerves and sharing a smile with Lydia, who'd put down her magazine. "Sorry, this has been a trying week. I'm a bit jumpy."

"Is there anything the church can help with?" Father Claudio asked.

"I'll be fine," Adam answered. Then he asked Lydia, "What's for dinner tonight?"

"You're a little early today, Dr. Calhoun," Lydia answered. "I was going to make your plate in a little bit. I'll get to it right now."

"Is the cafeteria closed to non-doctors?" Father Claudio asked Lydia.

"It's open to any friend of Dr. Calhoun's," Lydia said

with a smile. "I'll make two boxes." She turned her attention to Adam. "Do you want the Ruben pizza, or the German meatballs in sour cream?"

"I'll have the meatballs, please," Adam said.

"I'll have the same," Father Claudio added.

"OK," Lydia said, "meatballs it is. There ain't nothing wrong with the Ruben pizza, you know. One of these days I'm going to talk you into trying it."

"Maybe someday," Adam said with a chuckle. "Thousand Island dressing, corned beef and sauerkraut just does not sound good on a pizza to me."

"You need to try new things, Dr. Calhoun," Lydia said as she scooped two hefty portions of the meatball meal into the Styrofoam containers. "You just might like what you try. For dessert, we have some banana muffins. I made a batch special for the 'no nut' crowd. There's only one left. I hope you don't mind nuts in your muffin, Father. Dr. Calhoun can't have any in his, he's got a serious allergy."

"I actually prefer nuts in my muffin, thank you," Father Claudio answered.

"If it's not too much trouble, Lydia," Adam said, "Father and I would like to eat here."

"So you want your dinner on a plate?" Lydia asked.

"No," Adam answered. "I don't want to dirty any

144

dishes. I just mean that we'll be sitting at a table in the corner. Would that be okay, or do you have to close up?"

"Take all the time you need, Dr. Calhoun. I've got a lot of cleaning to do in the kitchen yet. I won't be going home for a while," Lydia said as she added a scoop full of cucumber salad to the containers, closed them and handed them over the glass sneeze guard.

Adam and Father Claudio took their boxes and placed them on the metal rail shelf in front of them. Lydia then turned to the glass cooler cabinet behind her and took out two cellophane-wrapped muffins and placed them in white paper sacks, folded the sacks closed and used a small piece of tape to seal the folds. She handed the sacks to Adam and Father Claudio, making sure that the right muffin went into the right hand. Adam led Father Claudio to the table in the corner where the Father had been waiting for Adam earlier. Adam set his dinner box on the table, and his paper sack containing his dessert at the edge of the table up against the wall.

"I'll be saving you for later," Adam said quietly as he set the sack down. "Father, would you care for a coffee or a juice?"

"No coffee for me, thanks," Father Claudio answered. "Caffeine makes me jittery. Some juice would be fine. Thank you."

Adam turned and headed towards the juice machine as Father Claudio set his meal down and seated himself at the table. Father Claudio then scanned the room. Lydia was back in the kitchen, and Adam was the only other soul in the room. Adam's attention was on the juice machine. Quickly, Father Claudio switched his muffin bag with Adam's and turned his attention to his own dinner.

muffin switch

A few moments later, Adam returned with two glasses of orange juice and sat at the table. He offered one glass to Father Claudio then opened his container, and, with a plastic fork that Lydia had provided, he began to eat his meal.

"I don't understand why the Vatican is so interested in this," Adam said.

"We're interested in your grandfather. He passed away, and then, days later, this girl, your patient, has a miraculous recovery," Father Claudio said. Then he took a bite of his meatball meal and let out a small moan of pleasure as he savored the flavor. "You must tell the cook what a wonderful job he, or she, has done. The food at the Vatican is quite nice, but this is just heavenly."

"I'll be sure to let her know," Adam said with a smile. He wondered just how good the Vatican food was if the priest had this reaction over hospital food. "How long have you been with the Vatican?" Adam asked.

"I worked at the Vatican as a lay person for many years then I migrated to the U.S. It was from here that I felt the call and returned to the Church. I applied to attend St. Thomas Aquinas Seminary in Missouri, but since I was older, I studied at a seminary in Illinois that had experience with older candidates. I could go on for years, but I'm afraid that I'm here to interview you. Your great-grandfather was not just a famous archeologist who lived a long life; he was an instrumental part of the Vatican's quest to gather not just artifacts but truths. I had the pleasure of meeting your great-grandfather on one of my first days at the Vatican many years ago. He was very kind."

"Thank you," Adam said. "What kind of information are you looking for?"

"I'll tell you what I know, and correct me if I'm wrong. Or, if you feel the need to add any information, please feel free to fill me in. I'm due to turn in my report in a few days. Your great-grandfather, Henry Calhoun, worked for the Vatican, and subsequently became a very wealthy man. He migrated to the U. S. in 1930. He met a woman and was married. In 1932, he had his only child, your grandmother Mae. She had three children; your mother Mary, your Aunt Helen, and your uncle Peter. He often quoted a verse about doing deeds. 'Do not speak about or tell of the deeds you do....do them without being noticed.'"

"Matthew," Adam said quietly with a warm smile of remembrance. "Take heed that you do not your alms before men, to be seen of them: otherwise you have no reward of your father which is within heaven. Therefore when you do your alms, do not sound a trumpet before you, as the hypocrites do in the synagogues and in the streets, that they may have glory of men. Truly I say to you, they have their reward. But when you do alms, let not your left hand know what your right hand does... I've read it. And yes, it was one of my papa's favorites. And his version was shorter."

Without being aware of it, while Adam recited the Bible verse, his right hand went to the silver crucifix hanging around his neck. He had put the necklace on earlier that morning because the slacks he was wearing didn't have a coin pouch in the front pocket, and Adam wanted to keep it on his person. Like before, once the necklace was around his neck, Adam had quickly forgotten he was wearing it. He had inadvertently lifted it out from under his shirt and rubbed it with his thumb in an automatic gesture.

"That's a very nice cross," Father Claudio said. Then, suddenly distracted, he added, "I'm sorry to cut the interview short, but I've just remembered something that I have to do before I retire for the evening. Perhaps we can pick this up in a couple of days. Enjoy your dinner." Father Claudio got up from the table abruptly, closed the Styrofoam container containing his meal and turned to leave.

"Don't forget your muffin," Adam called after the priest.

"Thank you, I wouldn't want to miss that," Father Claudio said as he scooped up his muffin sack from the table and hurried out of the cafeteria.

Adam took two more bites of his meatball dinner, and then decided to finish his dinner at home. He closed his dinner container, took the two half-empty glasses of orange juice to the dirty glass area and placed them in the tub. Adam noticed Lydia looking over at him as she was cleaning up. Adam waved.

"Bye now, Doc," she said with a hearty smile.

Adam smiled, took his dinner and dessert, and headed home for the evening.

Chapter 22.

Adam jiggled the door knob to his apartment. This was a recent ritual he found himself doing to ensure the door was as he left it that morning; locked. Satisfied the door had not been tampered with, Adam inserted his key and entered his apartment. Ever since he'd been attacked, Adam left the living room light on in an attempt to gain a sense of security in his mind by removing the element of surprise if someone was lurking about inside. He removed his coat and hung it on the coat rack attached to the wall by the door. He closed the door behind him, locking it and walked over to his kitchen to prepare a cup of black Irish tea.

A few minutes later, Adam emerged from the kitchen, tea in one hand and his bag containing his muffin in the other. He gently rested his cup of tea on his dining room table and plopped down on one of his scratched, mismatched dining room chairs that appeared to have been purchased at one of the local thrift shops. Adam tore the bag into two halves and used one half as a makeshift plate for his muffin. He lifted the moist muffin to his mouth and took a large bite, barely tasting the contents as he washed it down with a sip of his milk-infused tea. Without a second thought, he took another large bite of the muffin, this time, as he chewed the soft dessert, he crunched into an ingredient that his mind quickly identified as pecans.

Instant terror overcame Adam as he immediately spat out the nutty contents across the table. He quickly began unbuttoning his shirt with one hand and reached into his pocket, searching for an EpiPen with the other hand as he raced through his allergy action plan in his head. He waited and waited for the allergic shock his body would most certainly go into and require him to inject the epinephrine into his thigh but nothing happened. Surprised, Adam crumbled the muffin in his hand, searching for the culprit. As he broke the muffin apart within his fingers, one by one, finely chopped pecans came into view. Adam's heightened breathing had begun to settle down but he could not understand why he was not convulsing and in need of his EpiPen by now. This severe allergy was not something he had grown out of as he'd had an attack during his early days of medical school while eating a salad that had a raspberry walnut vinaigrette drizzled over it during a friend's social gathering.

Adam calmly began to button his shirt back up, and as he did, his hand brushed up against the crucifix that hung on the necklace his great-grandfather Henry had given him. The tiny hairs on his arms stood on end and he was overcome with a spooky yet strangely reassuring feeling but before he had a chance to further question the mysteries of the crucifix pendant, there was a knock on the front door. Adam was surprised to find Rose standing on his front stoop.

"I was just stopping by to check on you," Rose said. "I didn't get a call or text from you today and I wanted to make sure everything was all right."

"Why wouldn't everything be all right?" Adam asked suspiciously.

"We were supposed to meet for a late dinner, remember? Why are you looking at me like that?" Rose asked, feeling uncomfortable, as if she was the subject of an inquisition.

Adam stood stone-faced, still in shock as he clutched the pendant around his neck and worked on processing the information of what had just happened to him. Rose inched closer to him and gently lifted his chin up with her smooth hand, bringing the two eye to eye.

"What happened?" Rose asked, concerned, but in a comforting tone, revealing the impeccable bedside manner of a seasoned doctor.

Adam glanced over her shoulder, surveyed the area outside then placed his hand behind her back and gently pulled her inside the apartment. Rose took his hand from off her back and held it tightly in hers as she closed the door and walked him into the center of the living room. She glanced over to the dining room table where she could see the dissected corpse of a muffin and the spattered salvia-drenched crumbs strewn on the table.

"I'm surprised," Adam said, slightly out of breath.

"To see me?"

"No. Yes, I am. But no, I'm surprised I'm okay."

"You're not making any sense, Adam. Why don't you just tell me what happened?"

"That's just it. Nothing happened. I just ate a muffin with nuts and nothing. Nothing happened."

"You're freaking out over a muffin," Rose interjected, trying to make sense of his state of being without seeming insensitive. "Maybe you're really not allergic."

"No. I'm definitely allergic. I almost died in college.

That's how I met Tara. I fell on the floor in anaphylactic shock and she raced to my side. In a room full of soon-to-be-doctors, who stood staring over me helplessly, she raced to my side. Without a second thought, she started searching my pockets and found my EpiPen and injected me."

"Why don't you sit down? I will make you another cup of tea," Rose said.

Rose guided Adam over to the dining room table and sat him in a seat as she used the torn bag to wipe the table clean. She collected the scattered pieces of muffin in her hand and disappeared into the kitchen. Adam stretched his neck out, lifting his chin towards the ceiling and exhaled a deep calming breath then he lowered his head down to rest in the palms of his hands, elbows anchored on the table top.

Consumed by the disbelief of what had just occurred to him, Adam failed to notice a figure open his front door and slip inside the apartment. The figure walked toward Adam slowly but with purpose, stopping only a few feet from him. Adam raised his head, expecting to see Rose standing next to him with a fresh cup of tea, and sprang back in his chair, startled to find his cousin, Helen's youngest son, Jordy, standing only a few feet from him. Jordy was breathing short quick breaths and had beads of

Betrayel
by someone
close   good!

sweat forming on his temples.

"Jordy, hey—I, um..." Adam stammered.

Adam was completely taken back at the sight of his cousin. The two barely spoke at family gatherings and now Jordy was standing in his dining room in the middle of the night.

"Your front door was open," Jordy said anxiously as his hands fidgeted in the pockets of his wind breaker.

"Is everything all right? I don't think you've ever dropped by before," Adam said, trying to deflect the awkwardness of the moment.

Jordy's body shook nervously as he shifted his weight from side to side on the balls of his feet. Adam did his best to maintain eye contact with him. He wasn't sure, but it looked like his young cousin was under the influence of some kind of drug. Adam didn't have very much experience with people on drugs, but he had worked in the hospital long enough to hear plenty of stories, and he was starting to think that his cousin was on something.

Adam noticed Jordy's cheekbones were slightly more pronounced than he remembered. His face was thinner. His whole body was thinner. His unkempt hair, the slight scruff on his face, and the beginnings of dark circles around his wide bulging eyes gave Jordy the look of a madman.

155

"Jordy, calm down. What's going on?" Adam asked, trying to assess his cousin's condition.

"Give it to me!" Jordy fired off the words through his clenched teeth.

Jordy sprang onto Adam, gripping him by the throat and knocking him to the ground right out from his chair. Adam lay on the floor, choking from the grip his cousin had around his neck. He couldn't get enough breath to speak. Jordy's grip was tightening and Adam felt a sharp pain through his Adam's apple as though it was going to pop like a grape at any second. Adam tried pushing Jordy away, but his strength was leaving him as his whole body starved for oxygen. He felt light-headed as consciousness slipped away.

Jordy kept squeezing Adam's neck, waiting for the moment Adam's eyes would close so he could remove the necklace. Suddenly the shrill whistle of a tea kettle pulled Jordy's attention away from Adam. He looked over his shoulder towards the kitchen and instantly caught the cold gray underbelly of a soup pot squarely between his eyes.

THUD! The impact threw Jordy several feet away from Adam. When Jordy landed on his back, a shiny nickel-plated revolver fell out of his jacket pocket and slid across the floor. Rose stood between him and Adam, the

THE IRON RELIC BOOK I: THE CROSSING

handle of the soup pot clenched in both of her hands.

"Come on!" Rose shouted to Adam.

Rose dropped the soup pot onto the floor and helped Adam to his feet. As she got him up, Rose grabbed his hand and pulled him out of the apartment while Jordy writhed on the floor in a struggle to regain his bearings. Jordy clawed at his nose, sure it was broken from the collision with the wrong end of the soup pot and his eyes swelled with water. Adrenaline jolted through his body, sending it into auto-pilot, and he scrambled across the room for the gun. He dipped down, swooped up the weapon, and swerved unbalanced toward the front door in pursuit of Adam and Rose.

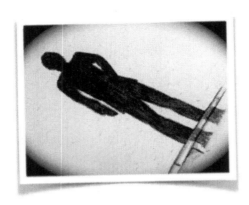

Chapter 23.

Adam and Rose rushed out of the apartment and onto the dimly lit street. They stopped in the street, a few feet from the sidewalk, next to Rose's car. Rose frantically fumbled through her pockets for her car keys as Adam anxiously kept watch on his front doorway. Rose quickly realized her keys were inside her purse, which was sitting on Adam's dining room table. She turned her attention back towards Adam.

"I left my keys inside," she said. The two exchanged glances and then focused back on the apartment in disbelief as Jordy stumbled through the doorway, gun in hand.

Jordy's vision slowly came back into focus and he spotted Adam near the sidewalk. He immediately raised the gun to fire at Adam, who froze, staring back blankly at the barrel of the gun like a deer trapped in the headlights of an oncoming semi-truck. Rose grabbed him by the upper arm and forcefully yanked him down the street. Frustrated, Jordy shoved the gun in his jacket pocket, grimaced at the headache that was mounting in his skull, and gave chase.

Adam and Rose ran west down the center of Corona Avenue. Adam's fear had begun to subside as his survival instincts kicked in and his mind was able to start analyzing the situation. He realized that they were exposed out in the open. Jordy could easily shoot them both in the back if he wanted to. Adam grabbed Rose's hand, reversing roles, and pulled her along as he turned right and ran between two parked cars and then through the yard that ran between the homes of two of his neighbors.

They ran side by side through the maze of suburban backyards and cul-de-sacs with Jordy inching his way closer and closer. Adam rounded an old metal trash bin and realized they were on the edge of a commercial neighborhood with shops and storefronts. Adam thought if he could lure Jordy into a populated area, he and Rose would be safe. Adam still had Rose's hand firmly grasped in his. They turned and ran into another side yard, heading straight for the back.

When Adam and Rose reached the five-foot-tall redwood fence that separated the backyard they were in from the alley behind it, Adam grabbed Rose by the waist and hoisted her over the fence in one move. Rose put out her hand to signal to Adam that she would help him over, but he had other plans.

"Rose, go that way," Adam panted, trying to catch his breath. He pointed to his right. "There is a bookstore and a coffee shop half a block away. It should still be open. Either that, or go to the convenience store."

"No, we stay together," Rose implored.

"Go!" Adam saw Jordy's silhouette against the house on the other side of the street in front of the house they had just run behind. "Now!"

Rose turned and ran down the alley in the direction Adam suggested. Adam turned to his left, leading Jordy in the opposite direction. Two yards over, Adam hurled himself over a small decorative white picket fence and into the alley. Beyond a garage, Adam ran into the street without looking for any traffic. He had entered the commercial neighborhood. It seemed oddly quiet. All of the shops were closed, and there were no cars or pedestrians in sight. It was later than he had realized.

Adam checked over his shoulder and saw Jordy hopping over the white picket fence he had just jumped

160

over. Adam continued running, leading Jordy down the alley, only this time, instead of garages and suburban backyards on either side, the alley was flanked by four-story brick buildings with rusty fire escapes bolted to their backs. Adam turned and ran into another small side alley in between two of the brick buildings. It was a grave mistake. This side alley was a dead end.

Adam spun himself around but it was too late. Jordy had caught up with him and was blocking his exit. Jordy raised the gun in his hand and aimed it to shoot Adam right between his eyes. The hammer on the gun was pulled back into the cocked position and Jordy's index finger was solid against the trigger.

"You don't need to do this," Adam said. He held his hands up to shoulder level with his palms out, showing Jordy that he was unarmed and willing to comply.

"All you had to do was give me the necklace, Adam," Jordy said with an eerie calmness. Adam saw that Jordy, being eight years younger than he, showed no signs of being winded. He was as steady and sure of himself as if he had just got up from the dinner table. Adam remembered going skeet shooting with Jordy and his brother Sean once. Jordy was a remarkable shot with a shotgun, and most likely he was equally as deadly with a pistol.

161

"OK, fine," Adam said as he pulled the necklace out from under his shirt, holding the crucifix pendant in his hand. "Look, we can go together to help your mom, I promise. Just put the gun down, Jordy." Adam took one step toward Jordy, holding the cross out in his hand as an offering. Jordy tightened his grip on the gun in a sign of distrust.

"I don't want to shoot you, Adam," Jordy warned. "

Adam continued to slowly creep towards his cousin, whose countenance suddenly shifted from the eerie calm predator into that of a jittery first-time hunter with buck fever as a bolt of adrenaline surged through his body. Beads of sweat slid down the handle of the gun as Jordy prepared to fire.

"Just give me the necklace!"

Bang! Bang! ... Bang!

Adam closed his eyes as every muscle in his body locked and tensed, bracing himself for the impact of a hot bullet. Jordy fell to his knees then onto his back. Blood ran from his chest, soaking his white windbreaker. A shocked look of disbelief was frozen onto his face. Adam rushed to his side to help him. He dropped to his knees and applied pressure to the wounds.

"Hold on!" Adam yelled.

"I just wanted it to help Mom," Jordy gurgled, gasping

for breath.

"Hold on. I'm going to get you help." Adam stuffed the necklace in his pocket and took out his cell phone to call 911. As Adam fumbled with the phone in one hand while keeping pressure on one of Jordy's wounds with the other, he heard a voice come from a shadow in the alley.

"Adam, it's going to be okay. I called 911. They're on the way." Out of the darkness, a figure emerged. Father Claudio was holding a cell phone in one hand and a gun in the other. "Are you, okay?"

"What kind of priest carries a gun?" Adam asked back, not believing his eyes.

"The Lord helps those who help themselves."

"You shot my cousin."

"I saved your life."

Adam turned to Jordy, shoved the cell phone back into his front pant pocket, and applied pressure with his free hand to another wound. "Hang in there, Jordy," Adam whispered as he continued emergency medical treatment.

Father Claudio raised his gun, aiming the barrel at the back of Adam's head. His plan was to shoot Adam in the back of the head, execution style, steal the necklace, and leave both bodies lying in the alley. But before he was able to pull the trigger, the sound of screeching tires punctured the air. A dark sedan with tinted windows smashed into Claudio, sending him flying over the hood of the car and onto the windshield. The car backed up, dumping his body onto the cement. Claudio cried out in pain.

Adam looked up, stunned in horror. Jordy clutched at Adam, struggling to cling to life. Adam looked down at his cousin, holding back tears at the sight of the blood bubbles boiling from Jordy's lips as he attempted to speak. The life slowly faded from Jordy's eyes. He died holding onto Adam's hands.

Police sirens blared in the distance, growing louder and louder. The door of the dark sedan opened, and the strange man who had followed Adam from Rose's duplex got out of the driver's seat. He was a tall thin man with white hair and blue eyes. He appeared to be in his mid- to late-fifties. The man, dressed in all black save the priest's collar that rested just below his pronounced Adam's apple, motioned with one hand for Adam to get into the car.

Adam pried his hands loose of his dead cousin's grip. He stood and suspiciously walked toward the dark sedan, making sure to keep an eye on Father Claudio, who was lying on the asphalt with his gun several feet in front of him. When Adam rounded the front of the car, instead of

164

getting in, he took off running down the alley. He ran faster than he'd ever run before. His feet could not even feel the pavement below them.

After several minutes, Adam found himself in the parking lot of a strip mall. Along one wall, between a sushi restaurant and a discount shoe store, there was a water fountain standing next to an old pay phone. Adam took a big long drink from the fountain in order to compose himself. He splashed water on his face and then washed the drying blood from his hands. As he was drying his hands on his pant legs, he felt a vibration in his pocket. Someone was calling his cell phone. He took out his cell phone to see that the incoming call was from an UNKNOWN CALLER.

"Hello?" Adam quietly said into the phone, keeping an eye on the parking lot and the street ahead of him.

"I need you to listen very carefully right now." The voice on the phone was one that Adam recognized as one of the men who had broken into his house and assaulted him. "The next few moments are going to change your life forever. Good or bad, it's up to you. Rose is with us."

"Who is this?" Adam gasped. "What do you want?"

"Right now, Doctor, I suggest you shut up and allow me to finish. She is with us and eager to leave. In what manner she leaves is up to you, Doctor. Are you following me?"

"Yes," Adam replied, defeated.

"Good. Then do exactly as I say. In precisely three hours, I want you to meet us at 357 Cornerstone Valley. It's in the abandoned train yard. When you get there, I will call you and instruct you where to go. Make sure you have that shiny necklace of yours." Click. The phone went silent.

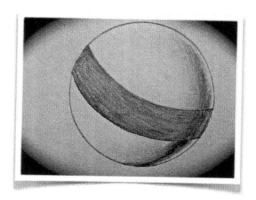

Chapter 24.

Pete was wearing sweat pants and a short-sleeved, solid grey polo-style shirt with dark, chocolate-colored moccasin-style slippers when he unlocked and opened the solid wood door to find Adam standing outside the mansion, still ringing the doorbell. Adam's hands were shaking uncontrollably and his teeth chattered from the cold night air. His body temperature was dropping from the damp bloodstains that covered the front of his shirt.

"Adam. Oh my God, is that blood?" Pete rushed Adam inside the mansion, closing the door behind them. "Are you okay? Do you need me to call 911? What happened?"

"No, no... I need your help."

"Let's talk in the other room." Pete motioned for Adam to follow him into the billiards room across the foyer. Adam followed after Pete and started rattling off what happened to Jordy and Rose.

Several minutes later, Pete was standing next to his wet bar, fixing Adam a drink to calm his nerves. Adam stood restless next to the billiard table with a throw blanket draped over his shoulders.

"I don't know what I'm supposed to do," Adam said, holding back the tears that were welling up in his eyes.

"You call the cops and you let them handle it. I feel bad for your girlfriend Rose, but, Adam...this is no time to be a hero. Your cousin is dead. Who knows how many people are after you — we need to get you to a safe place, and you need to keep a low profile," Pete said in a firm tone. He approached Adam with an amber colored drink in a crystal snifter. "Here, have a drink. This will heat your bones and calm your nerves. I want you to sit down and let's just take a second to analyze the situation."

Adam took the drink, downing it in one gulp. Pete placed his arm around the young doctor and guided him towards the dark brown leather sofa.

"Uncle Pete, I can't let anything happen to Rose," Adam said as the guilt grew inside him.

"There's nothing you can do," Pete replied in an attempt to resign Adam to the situation.

"I—I..." Adam's tongue felt heavy and disconnected. His eyeballs seemed to whirl inside their sockets as he grasped for consciousness. As he staggered to the couch, the young doctor knew that he had been drugged.

Chapter 25.

Adam's eyes fluttered as he came to. A yellow halo from one of the recessed lights above him pierced his eyelids, helping to restore his consciousness. In the background, Adam could hear the cracking of pool balls. He stretched out his right arm, grabbed the back of the couch and gingerly pulled himself to a half-seated position from where he could see Pete playing a game of solo nine ball. A shot of fear pulsed through his veins as he instantly reached into his pockets. The necklace was gone. Adam frantically searched the couch where he was lying but nothing was to be found.

"The necklace is in a safe place," Pete said reassuringly.

"Rose is going to die over this!" Adam said as he checked the time on his wristwatch. Over an hour had passed since he'd arrived at Uncle Pete's mansion.

"Self-preservation, Adam. There are always sacrifices that must be made in life," Pete said stoically as he sank the four-ball into the side pocket with one fluid stroke of the pool stick.

"Why would you do this?" Adam asked. Betrayal surged through his heart.

"I'm your godfather, Adam. Some people don't take that role very seriously but I do. Since your mother died, I've always seen you as part of my responsibility. This is what she would want me to do. Your phone is over there if you want to call the police to help your girlfriend. But as for the necklace, you might as well forget you ever laid eyes on it."

Adam rose to his feet, slowly finding his balance. He steadied himself as he prepared to rush out of the room.

"Adam, think!" Pete barked from across the billiard table.

"Weak men choose to stand by in the face of evil, strong men choose to stand in front of it," Adam said defiantly.

"Those are the words of your great-grandfather," Pete said quietly. "Adam, you won't get there on foot."

"I have to try."

Pete clenched his jaw and shook his head in disbelief

at what he was about to do. "Wait. Here." He walked over to an ashtray on the wet bar, retrieved the keys it contained, and tossed them over to Adam, who caught them. Adam nodded in thanks, picked up his cell phone and hurried out of the room.

Pete waited a moment until he was confident that Adam had left the mansion, and then picked up his cell phone from the end table. He wandered over to the window and watched as Adam rushed into the circular driveway towards the 2014 Black Audi A8 parked outside. Pete slid his finger across the screen of his cell phone to reveal the keypad and began to dial.

The call was answered with a single word. "Yes."

"He's on his way. Leave the girl. I have the necklace."

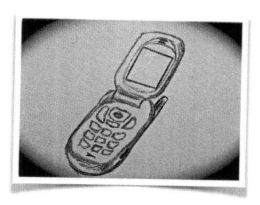

Chapter 26.

Rose opened her eyes as she felt the blindfold that was wrapped tightly around her head being removed. Her eyes took a moment to focus. She looked around the large empty room and assumed that she must be in an empty warehouse somewhere near the industrial district. The large empty room had high windows, approximately three stories in the air. The concrete floors and cinderblock walls were scarred with peeling paint and years of weathering. Every twenty feet or so, there was a metal post that rose to the high wooden ceiling. Rose found herself tied to one of these posts with a dry frayed length of hemp rope. A salty handkerchief smelling of old sweat was tied tightly across her mouth as a gag.

The two burly kidnappers who had grabbed Rose and knocked her out at the end of the alleyway were standing on either side of her. Both men were wearing ski masks and dark clothing. Rose thought they must have got the idea of how to dress like burglars from a Disney cartoon. The taller one of the two was on her left, and was holding a cell phone to his ear. The other one was standing inches from her, his eyes examining her as if he'd never stood that close to a woman before. He was holding a large knife. The large kidnapper hung up his cell phone and put it inside his coat pocket.

"Time to go," the large kidnapper said as he slid his cell phone into his jacket pocket. The voice was that of Hiram Grey's.

"What about the woman?" Horace asked, keeping his favorite companion, his knife, trained on Rose's neck.

"The old man says to leave her. He has the item," Hiram said as he turned to walk toward the large loading door at the end of the room.

Horace leaned in to Rose and raised his mask from under his chin to the ridge of his nose, exposing his nostrils. He inhaled deeply as he smelled Rose's neck, sending a chill down her spine. "That's too bad," he said as he replaced his mask. "I was planning on having some real fun with her."

"Look," Hiram said as he spun around and quickly advanced on his smaller brother. He grabbed Horace by

174

his collar and pulled him back several feet from Rose. "Don't screw this up! The plan was simple and it's working. We tricked the old man into hiring us to help him find the necklace. It's not exactly the way we planned it, but the old man has the necklace. So, we go to him to get paid, we take our money, we knock him around a little, and we take the necklace. Then we deliver the necklace to the boss and we get paid again. It's what I call a win-win. Don't mess things up by getting sloppy and stupid." Hiram let go of his brother's collar and turned to leave.

"Too bad we don't get to play, little lady," Horace said to Rose. "You look like you would be real fun."

Bang! A gunshot rang out. Horace spun away from Rose to find his brother's lifeless body lying on the floor. A second flash of fire spat out of the barrel of a black 9mm handgun just beyond the open doorway leading into the darkness. The bullet dropped Horace instantly. The shot echoed throughout the warehouse. Fear flushed Rose's face, horror and tears of panic streamed down her cheeks as she pulled at her ropes to free herself.

"Calm down," shouted a voice from beyond the open doorway where the shots had come from. "Everything in life has an antithesis. What once was lost will be found again. We are of the same flesh."

Rose slowly settled down as she heard the words. They reverberated through her mind and triggered her training to kick in. She recognized the code of the organization she worked for; the organization she was born into and lived to serve. She had always received her orders in the United States from an unknown source in coded messages. Sometimes the code would come in the form of a text message, sometimes an email or an ad in a daily newspaper, but she had never met another member face to face in the field. She knew there was another operative working collectively with her—she just never knew who it was, until now.

A steady hand reached across her mouth, gripped the sweat-soaked gag and pulled it down under her chin. Her hands were untied. She turned to face her rescuer. She had seen this man before. The other operative working with her to retrieve the artifact was the priest who had approached Adam during the museum dedication for Henry Calhoun, the same man who had introduced himself as Father Claudio. His pants and shirt were torn and dirty and a thin trail of blood was leaking from his leg.

"You!" Rose said, not able to hide the surprise in her voice.

The man winced in pain as he took an awkward step

backward to quickly regain his balance. His injuries were more serious than just a scratched leg.

"Let me take a look at your leg," Rose said, her medical training taking over.

"We don't have time," Claudio said. "Our superiors are going to eliminate both of us if we don't take care of business. What happened in the apartment? Didn't he eat the –"

"Yes," Rose interrupted. "He should have gone into anaphylactic shock."

"He was wearing the cross, wasn't he?"

"Yes."

"Then the myths are true."

"I heard one of the men say that an old man has the necklace. Who?"

"Someone else has the cross now? I need you to find Adam and finish this."

"It's too messy—he's going to want to call the police."

"Work it out," Claudio snapped while he pulled a small cell phone from his jacket pocket. "Find out where the necklace is and once you do, use this phone and call the number programmed into the speed dial. I'll take care of the rest from there. We don't have much time before they send someone to replace us. This is starting to get out of control, and they don't allow situations to get out of control."

"What about Adam?" Rose asked, trying to mask the genuine concern she felt for her mark. She had never gotten emotionally connected to a target before but she knew that she must not allow herself to appear compromised to Claudio.

"You get the privilege of taking care of him yourself," Claudio answered with a sinister smile.

"If we get the necklace, there's no reason to harm him," Rose replied. She instantly regretted her suggestion. In this simple comment she may have revealed her feelings for Adam, which would mean certain death for them both if Claudio suspected anything. Rose hoped she hadn't just betrayed herself and waited for Claudio's reaction.

"That's not our decision to make," Claudio said, no longer smiling. "There's no going back. You know that."

Rose nodded her head, signaling her understanding. She gathered her composure and headed out of the warehouse. Claudio watched her leave with a suspicious eye. He limped over to the door and watched as Rose stumbled out into the night. He stepped back inside the warehouse and closed the door. He reached into his pocket and removed his cell phone. His pointy fingers dialed a number and then perched the phone to his ear.

"She is on her way back to the doctor. I fear she has lost her way."

"Remove Rose from the equation as soon as you recover the necklace," the voice on the other end of the phone replied in a heavy Baltic accent.

"And the doctor, Adam? If she doesn't kill him?" Claudio asked.

"No survivors. Everything in life has an antithesis."

"What once was lost will be found again," Claudio answered as he hung up.

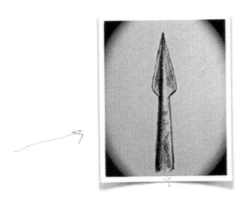

Chapter 27.

Adam slowly drove Pete's Audi through the isolated, gravel-strewn train yard, looking for any signs of life. There was a light mist in the air, making it difficult to see more than eight or ten feet in front of the car by Adam's best estimate. With the front windows rolled down and his radio off, Adam listened desperately for a noise that would give him Rose's position. All of his senses were on high alert. The cool night air smelled crisp and oddly clean, although a faint underlying smell of industrial grade grease was a constant presence. The popping noise of gravel being slowly ground into dust under the weight of the car was the only noise Adam could hear. He navigated the car through massive steel shipping crates. As he circled the car into an empty clearing, he saw a figure running in his direction. He clicked on his high beams to get a better look. Arms were thrown up in reaction to the blinding light.

Adam unbuckled his safety belt and allowed it to slide back into its retractor then leaned to his left and stuck his head out through the open window to get a better look. He slowly realized that the figure standing in front of his car was Rose. Adam slammed the gear shift into the park position and rushed out of the car. He ran up to Rose and held her tightly in his arms. He could feel the tears that had been streaming down her bruised face against his own.

"Rose! Thank God I found you," Adam whispered into her ear.

"Adam, we need to go," Rose said as she sank into his arms. Almost losing her balance on the loose gravel under her feet, Rose put her right hand on Adam's chest and her left hand grabbed his right arm. Adam helped Rose into the car.

Once they were safely out of the train yard, Adam turned on the car's interior light and saw the extent of the bruises on Rose's face.

"Are you okay?" Adam gasped. "We need to get you to the hospital."

"No!" Rose snapped. Then she regained her composure. "No. I'm fine. Just a little bruised. Just drive." Rose turned in her seat, stealing a glance at Adam and then stared out the back window of the car.

"Are they following us?" Adam asked, hoping the answer would be no.

"I don't know," Rose answered. "I don't think so."

"I am so sorry, Rose. This is all my fault."

Rose righted herself in her seat and took a deep breath. She put her head in her hands for a moment, but the pain from her bruises on her face kept her focused. "What did they want?" Rose asked. "The man at your apartment said he wanted a necklace. Why?"

"My great-grandfather's necklace," Adam answered. He wanted to unburden himself and tell Rose everything, but just as he was about to reveal the whole history of the relic inside the necklace and how it may have healing powers, he noticed that something didn't feel right. Maybe now wasn't the right time, he thought to himself. Instead, all he said was, "It doesn't matter. I don't have it anymore."

"You gave it to him?" Rose asked.

"No. Uncle Pete. He... It doesn't matter." The mixed emotions welled up inside of Adam and his voice cracked as he fought back tears. "None of this matters. I was so afraid I was going to lose you. We have to call the police."

"No, Adam, please—not yet. They threatened to kill

us if we called the police. Please, let's just leave town for a few days. Please." Rose lost control of her emotions and tears streamed down her face again.

"Okay," Adam said softly, not able to stand the sight of her crying. He gently touched her face with his palm. Adam saw the bright lights of a gas station with a convenience store ahead of them on the corner of the next block. With a flick of his left hand, Adam turned on the car's turn signal. The car slowed as he carefully pulled into the gas station and parked at one of the pumps.

"I'll just be a second," he said as he unbuckled his safety belt. He opened the door and got out, looking back in the direction of the train yard. Once he was satisfied that no one had been following them, he closed the driver's side door and quickly walked into the station.

Rose followed Adam with her eyes as he walked inside the convenience store. As the store door swung closed behind him, Rose took out the cell phone Claudio had given her and quickly searched the contact phone book. There was only one number programmed into the phone. She clicked SEND TEXT. She began typing. "Necklace Found. With Adam's Uncle Pete. At his home." She shot a quick look back towards the convenience store and saw Adam paying the cashier then looked back down at the phone and stared at the message, mulling over all of the ramifications of her actions if she failed to send this message. If she sent it, Pete would surely die. If she failed to send it, both she and Adam would most likely become hunted like stray dogs in a Third World country. She took a deep breath, and pressed SEND.

Adam walked briskly out of the convenience store, carrying a map under his arm. The cool night air blew into his back as he glanced cautiously in all directions on his way to the car. When he got inside, he opened the map across the steering wheel.

"Looks like we can take I-70 over the Nelson Bridge," Adam said. "That'll take us to Crowne County. My family has a cabin there we haven't used in years. It's pretty remote. We can lay low there for a few days. That should give us a chance to figure out what we're going to do." Adam took out his cell phone and scrolled through his contacts.

"Who are you calling?" Rose asked.

"Uncle Pete," Adam answered. "I need to let him know what's going on, and have him call Aunt Helen to tell her about Jordy."

"Do you think that's a good idea? What if they are tracing your cell phone?"

"I can't have my cousin's body lying in some alley."

"You said you heard police sirens before you fled,

184

right?" Rose took Adam's hand in hers and gave it a reassuring squeeze. "I'm sure someone heard the gunshots and called 911."

Adam looked into Rose's eyes and thought for a moment. What she was saying made sense. Surely the police had been called and Jordy's body discovered. He had most likely already been identified, and an officer was on his or her way to Aunt Helen's house. Adam put his cell phone back into his pocket. He folded the map back up and put it in the console then he put the key in the ignition and started the car.

The cell phone in Rose's lap lit up. She quickly clicked the end button, but noticed it was an incoming text message. The text read: "On my way. Finish the job."

"We should get going," Rose said as she tucked the cell phone back into her pocket.

Adam put the car in gear and drove out of the parking lot and onto the frontage road. Rose stared out of the car window in hopeless agony. She tried to remain composed, recalling that her mission was to eliminate Adam.

"I bet you never thought this was what you were signing up for," Adam said, trying to break the silence between them.

"What?" Rose asked. She was distracted by the nature of Adam's comment. Did he know about her? Had he suspected that she had been trying to locate the necklace the whole time, ever since Henry's death? Was he referring to his dead cousin, or was he referring to the torture she had just endured? All of these questions instantly raced through her mind.

"I was just kidding— I do that when I get nervous. I was just trying to say that I bet this isn't what you thought was going to happen with us back when you asked me out to dinner."

"Right." Rose sighed with relief.

"I'm so sorry I got you involved in all of this. I had no idea any of this would happen. Everything feels so surreal. This just doesn't happen to everyday people. I don't understand any of it. I just wanted to spend my life helping people. That's it. I wanted to be a small town doctor, with a simple life. And I feel like I've put my whole family in danger over something that wasn't even mine to begin with. If I'd given the necklace to Jordy, he might still be alive and you would not have gone through any of this."

"You can't blame yourself for everything that might go wrong around you. That's not your cross to bear," Rose said, comforting him.

"Have you ever done something so bad, one moment in your life, you just wish you could take back?"

186

"I have."

"I wish I could start over and just bury that necklace with Papa Henry."

"Henry was so proud of you. He raved about you every day I saw him."

"He was just hoping to get a great-great-grandchild out of me before he died. When I was dating Tara, he used to buy us these expensive romantic vacations just hoping that one of them would inspire me to propose to her. He said, 'If you got a gal you love, it's simple. You look her in the eyes and you say, I love you and you are going to be my wife.'" Adam chuckled and glanced at Rose. She glanced back into Adam's eyes, taken by him. The moment sauntered into romantic territory before Rose cautiously looked away.

"What if she said no?" Rose asked.

"That's the thing —he said once you looked her in the eyes, she would never say no."

"Why is that?"

"Because she would see truth in your eyes."

"Was it easy for you to propose?" Rose asked.

"Yeah, it was. I did it in Corfu, Greece. She said yes, and a week later, she died. We were in our last year of medical school. She was riding her bike to class when a car lost control and skidded over into the bike lane. I was supposed to pick her up that morning but... well." Adam continued to tell the tale even though tears had welled up in his eyes and sadness had covered his face. "That's the type of guilt that stains you for life. I never saw faith the same way again after that. Sometimes in life we just have no opportunity to ask for forgiveness from the people we lose."

"My mother used to tell me the story of Saul, the greatest sinner that ever lived. He spent his early life persecuting the disciples of Jesus and one day on his journey to Damascus, he was struck down blind by a great light and fell to his knees before a resurrected Jesus, who asked Saul, 'Why do you persecute me?' Trembling, Saul asked the Lord what he would have him do. Jesus sent him into the city where three days later his sight was restored. My mom would finish the story by saying to me no matter how much you feel you'd turned your back on the ones you love, there's always forgiveness."

Adam took in what Rose said to him in for a moment, checked the mirrors to ensure a safe lane change then passed the silver Volkswagen Passat that had been in front of them, driving exactly two miles an hour under the speed limit for the last ten miles.

"I am truly grateful to have you in my life, Rose," Adam said. "Maybe all of this was meant to be, and the necklace is in the right hands now."

Rose looked out of the passenger window, disgust with herself growing in her heart. Guilt had overcome her as her mother's story sank into her soul. It was one of the few stories her mother had shared with her growing up.

"Adam, I need you to listen to me. Your uncle is in danger," Rose suddenly blurted out, her conscience winning out.

Adam glanced at her with a quizzical look on his face. Rose's inner attitude spewed to the surface as she began talking quickly and with purpose.

"You need to call your uncle. I need you to tell him to get out of his house and go to the police."

"Rose, slow down," Adam said, confused. "What are you talking about?"

"The two men who kidnapped me. I overheard them saying that they knew where it was. I didn't put two and two together until now, but I think they are going after the necklace. If your Uncle Pete has the necklace, then he's in danger."

Adam hit the brakes and pulled over to an abrupt stop on the side of the road. The silver Passat swerved to the left lane, tires screeching and horn blowing in loud objection to Adam's driving. Adam pulled his cell phone out from his pocket and began to dial his uncle's number.

The phone rang and rang, but no one answered.

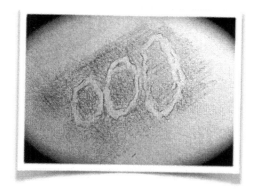

smoke rings

Chapter 28.

In the billiards room of his mansion, Pete carefully poured himself a splash of a velvety bronze cognac into a sparkling clean glass snifter. He methodically swirled the cognac, creating a gentle whirlpool within his glass then he brought the snifter to his nose, allowing the floral notes to invade his nostrils before pouring the sample down his gullet. He released a smile of pure delight and failed to notice that his cell phone was vibrating across the room as it rested on the billiard table.

Pete set his snifter down on his wet bar and opened a humidor that was built directly underneath. He whistled to himself as he removed a fine hand-rolled cigar from its soft cream felt resting place. Pete held the cigar up, gently gliding it under his nose as he savored the smell. This moment was one he had been waiting for for a long time.

The past thirty-seven years to be exact, dating all the way back to the moment when his grandpa Henry had chosen him to be the heir apparent to the silver crucifix necklace. However, once Pete's sister Mary became pregnant with Henry's first great-grandson, Adam, that all changed. But now, none of that mattered, Pete thought to himself as he clipped off the end of the cigar. He turned his attention back to the beautifully crafted, crystal decanter containing the Leopold Gourmel Quintessence 30 Carats cognac, removed the crystal stopper, and poured himself a glass three fingers high. He carefully rolled his cigar between his forefinger and thumb then dipped the end of the cigar into his drink before finally placing the walnut colored cigar between his lips and lighting it. Pete then tilted his head back, looking toward the ceiling as he blew out a thick ring of smoke that slowly dissipated as it tunneled out in diameter up into the air. The smoke waded across the room and swept past the billiards table where the cell phone had fallen silent. The small blue light on the phone blinked repeatedly as it signaled several missed call notifications.

**

Adam slammed his cell phone down onto the car's center console in anger and disbelief. With his left hand, he wiped the sweat from his face. He could feel his heart rate increasing and he was breathing more heavily than normal. Rose looked at him with a confused and frightened expression on her face.

"I keep getting his voicemail," Adam said. "We have to go back."

Adam turned the car around, driving over the grassy median that separated the eastbound and westbound lanes of Interstate 70; his tires spinning and kicking up dirt and grass as they cut ruts through it. As the car sped back towards town, Adam picked up his cell phone and started dialing the police, in spite of Rose's warnings.

"Maybe he's in the bathroom or something," Rose said, trying to calm Adam down.

"I'm calling the police. I should've called them in the first place. I'm going to drop you off at the hospital. You'll be safe there. I don't want you getting into any more danger."

"Adam, I'm with you," Rose said with a renewed determination in her voice. "Period."

***

Pete reclined in a black leather armchair in the billiards room of his mansion, swirling his cognac in his glass in his right hand, savoring his victory in collecting the necklace from Adam. The recessed lights were dimmed down to a more relaxing and darker hue.

A man's voice seeped out of the darkness from behind Pete. "Congratulations on obtaining the necklace. Now, if you'll just hand it over, I'll be on my way."

Pete spun out of his chair, startled by the intruder and stared at the intimidating figure cloaked in a priest's attire. Claudio was standing in the doorway, gun leveled on Pete in his right hand, his left arm holding his broken ribs tightly. Claudio was still bleeding slightly from a wound on his head and his garb was tattered after his run-in with the car.

"Who are you? How did you get in here?" Pete snarled defiantly.

"Just give me the necklace," Claudio instructed, his voice in a slow simmer.

"I don't know what you're talking about. Now get out of my house!"

"Don't push me, Mr. Mitchell. I don't have the patience for it today. Just give me the necklace."

"I swear I don't know....."

"Mr. Mitchell, I know that you stole the necklace from your nephew Adam just a short while ago. Do not test me." Claudio fired a warning shot into the ceiling directly above Pete. The bullet exploded through one of the recessed light bulbs, raining down shards of glass on Pete's head.

194

"I don't have it! Adam wouldn't turn it over! He said that he hid it somewhere!"

"You're a terrible liar, Mr. Mitchell. I'll give you to the count of three to put the necklace in my hand. One...."

"If I had it, I'd give it to you, but I ..."

"Two..."

"I'm telling the truth! Adam came by earlier, but he didn't have it on him..."

Claudio fired a shot directly into Pete's stomach. Pete crumpled over, falling to the floor in anguish. He grasped his stomach in an attempt to stop the wound from bleeding out on the floor.

"Three." Claudio finished the countdown as he limped over to the chair where Pete had been sitting. He slowly sat down as he watched Pete dragging himself toward the billiard table.

"A gut shot is a slow and very painful way to die, Mr. Mitchell. Too bad for you your nephew, the doctor, isn't here to save you. I guess you'll just have to pray for a miracle," Claudio sneered.

Pete reached the billiard table and stretched his arm toward the side pocket. He managed to slide his fingers underneath the pocket and push a hidden button with the last of his might to reveal a secret compartment in the side of the table. The necklace was resting inside that compartment. Pete reached into the compartment and grabbed the necklace. He pressed the necklace against the wound on his stomach and began to pray.

Claudio watched Pete, amused by the spectacle, but now was the time for him to collect his prize. He stood up from the chair with a groan, eyeing Pete. "You see, Mr. Mitchell, I knew you were lying. Didn't anyone ever tell you that lying was a sin?" Claudio approached Pete, bent down and firmly pried the necklace from Pete's fingers.

As Claudio straightened himself up, he felt a swift lightning strike of pain in his rib cage as he was suddenly knocked off his feet. Adam squeezed his arms around Claudio with all his might as he tackled the man to the ground.

Claudio clawed at Adam's face with one hand, trying to strike him in the delicate tissue around his eyes as he lifted the gun with his other hand towards Adam's temple. Adam grabbed Claudio by the wrists and slammed Claudio onto his back, forcing the man to drop his gun. Rose rushed to Adam's side, grabbed the gun and stepped backwards several feet from the entangled men. Adam wrestled the necklace from Claudio, kneeing the assassin in his damaged ribs and causing him to gasp for air in the process. Adam rose to his feet victorious, necklace in hand and intact with the silver crucifix pendant. He rushed to Pete's side. Adam placed the crucifix in Pete's hand and began to pray over him, taking his focus off Claudio.

Claudio lay on the floor and watched Rose intently as she aimed the gun at him. He waited patiently for the slightest opportunity to pounce. And then, it happened. Her head giving way to her heart, Rose took her eyes off him for a millisecond as she crossed over to check on Adam. Claudio seized his moment and pulled a second pistol from his sock holster. Claudio leveled the pistol at Rose's back as she crossed between Adam and Claudio.

Rose turned to Claudio just as he squeezed the trigger on the pistol. She shifted her body to the side. The bullet tore into Rose's hip, dropping her to the floor. As she fell to the ground, Rose fired back, shooting Claudio center mass. Adam turned to find Rose lying on the floor behind him. He pulled her closer, wrapped the necklace around her and Pete's clasped hands, and continued to pray.

Rose grabbed Adam by the cheek; making eye contact with him, she said, "Adam, call 911." Her weak voice crumbled in pain.

Chapter 29.

Adam dropped his cell phone after confirming the address with the 911 operator and returned his focus onto praying for Pete and Rose. Adam felt Pete try to push the necklace away. Adam pressed it back into his hand, but Pete shook his head and pushed it along with Adam's hands onto Rose.

"I'm sorry, Adam," Pete said softly.

"Shush, don't talk," Adam told Pete as tears stormed in his eyes. "The ambulance is coming. It's going to be okay."

Pete shook his head and coughed. A slight trickle of blood flowed from the corner of his mouth. His eyes focused onto Adam as he labored for breath. With one hand on his wound, he used the other to grab Adam's arm and he held onto it tightly.

"I need you to know that I've done some terrible things. I've been foolish and selfish, Adam, but amidst all of my stupidity, I've always loved my family."

"Don't talk now, save your strength," Adam replied as he continued pressing the crucifix pendant onto Rose's hip.

"Adam, listen to your uncle," Rose said. "Let him talk if he wants to."

Adam realized that he was losing his uncle. Pete was slowly fading away. A feeling of great sadness overcame Adam. He nodded his head and held Pete's hand tightly.

"I caused Helen's blindness," Pete confessed. "It's not her diabetes at all. It was simple really; we all know how much Helen drinks, even though she's not supposed to. I cut her liquor bottles with methanol and a touch of formaldehyde. That's what induced her blindness."

"What? Why?" Adam asked, shocked at what he was hearing.

"I thought she had the necklace. I thought that if she needed it, she would reveal its whereabouts. But then, when you told me that you had it, I sent Jordy to get it from you. I thought he could convince you to let Helen use it. I never meant for anyone to get hurt. I was weak. Forgive me?"

"I do," Adam said.

Pete closed his eyes. A sense of calm overtook him as Adam's words of forgiveness settled his soul. Pete's grip on Adam's arm loosened as his life slipped away from his body.

"No, hang on, Uncle Pete. Hang on," Adam demanded, as he struggled to apply pressure on the gunshot wound. But it was too late. Pete's body had gone cold from shock. He let out one last breath and then died. Adam gathered up his uncle's body in both of his arms and held him tight, sobbing. Rose was able to sit herself upright on the floor and watch with both a sense of guilt at the role she had played in this and the fear of what more was to come.

Time seemed to pause for Adam. He heard each wail as if in slow motion, his body had gone completely numb from adrenaline and despair. Pete had been a second father to him growing up and now all of the men Adam admired and felt he understood, were gone, leaving him alone. Where was the faith Henry had spoken of? Where was the comfort in his time of need?

"God, where are you?" slipped from Adam's mouth, barely audible.

Just then, Adam felt his body warm. The thickness of the room dissipated. Adam's closed eyelids felt a glow grow upon them. The darkness he saw was suddenly broken by the pouring in of golden light. He witnessed in his mind's eye a pair of strong golden arms swoop in to embrace him and Pete. Comfort and peace filled Adam's soul like a flood of hope and love. His tears dried and he slowly opened his eyes. As he did, he saw a ray of light shine through the east facing window, piercing the fleeting night. The heavenly light seemed to be a spotlight from God, focused on the two men. And just as soon as it had appeared, the iris of the clouds closed around the light, shrinking it until the only light that remained shone directly on Henry's necklace and the crucifix pendant lying in Adam's blood-drenched hand.

Adam knew that what he had been missing had been restored. He was not alone. A father was with him, the Father. The corners of his mouth rose gently into a slight smile of acknowledgment and the healing light faded out. Adam knew what had to be done.

Chapter 30.

Thirty minutes later, Adam found himself seated in the back seat of Detective Tarsus' black 2013 Crown Victoria that served as the detective's unmarked police car. From out of the window to his right, Adam could see the red and blue flashing lights from the other police cars and ambulances illuminate the exterior of his late uncle's mansion and landscaping in a strange and moving sort of way. A uniformed police officer finished stretching crime scene tape across the entryway of the mansion as the coroner and his assistant wheeled the body of the man who called himself Father Claudio out in a body bag on a gurney and parked it next to the gurney that held the body of Adam's uncle. Rose was seated in the back of an ambulance being assisted by a medic while another officer questioned her about the evening.

Sitting next to Adam in the back seat of his own unmarked police car was Detective Hiro Tarsus. He was quickly scribbling away in his small pocket-sized notebook, making sure he gathered the information that Adam had just detailed out for him. Detective Tarsus was a first generation American. His parents migrated from Japan to America in the early 1970s and gained citizenship while working for an electronics manufacturing company. Hiro was born into a home with both American and Japanese values, traditions, and language. Although he was forty years old, his slender six-foot-tall frame, black hair, dark brown eyes and smooth clear complexion deceived the eye. Even though he attempted to look older with the allowance of what little facial hair that would grow above his upper lip and on his chin, Hiro Tarsus had the appearance of a thirty-year-old. Some would call the good-looking detective's age-defying appearance a blessing, but the man himself viewed it as a curse.

Few people respect a boyish face, even if it is wearing a detective's badge, Hiro had learned. His devilish good looks and his Japanese parents had given Hiro cause to work very hard at everything he had earned in life. He was a very good, detail-oriented detective; a well-trained officer of the law. He excelled in all areas of law enforcement, including marksmanship. Before he received his combat training from the police force, Hiro's mother and father ensured he could defend himself by making sure their son was trained in Judo, Kendo and Aikido in addition to Karate. Hiro's mother also insisted he be trained in the philosophical concept of Aiki, a philosophy of joining energy; the principal of matching one's opponent in order to defeat them.

Hiro had not expected he would be interviewing a doctor concerning a double homicide when he'd started his shift an hour before.

"Thank you for your statement Dr. Calhoun," Detective Tarsus said as he closed his notebook and placed it and his short pencil into his jacket pocket. "Now let me make sure I've got this right. You're saying that your great-grandfather gave you a necklace. And some people think this necklace may be extremely old and valuable."

"Something like that," Adam replied, his gaze still fixed on Rose.

"Okay. Your apartment gets ransacked, and you get mugged. And you think the muggers were after the necklace. Then your cousin tries to steal the necklace from you, and in that altercation, your cousin is shot and killed by a man dressed as a priest. Your uncle drugs you

204

and steals the necklace. Then Dr. Powell is kidnapped, and you go to rescue her. Then the man dressed as a priest comes here and shoots your uncle to get the necklace from him. You and Dr. Powell come here to get the necklace back; there's a struggle and Dr. Powell is shot, and the man dressed as a priest is killed. Did I miss anything?"

"No," Adam said, "that just about sums it up."

"So where's the necklace now?"

"I have it."

Just then a uniformed police officer came over to the detective and whispered something in his ear. Detective Tarsus thanked the officer and returned to Adam.

"It appears that the deceased priest isn't a priest at all. No surprise there. What is a surprise is that the man has had his fingerprints removed. No ID and no serial numbers on the guns in his possession. This bothers me. Dr. Calhoun, I think that as long as you're in possession of that necklace, you and everyone around you are in danger."

"Aunt Helen..." Adam gasped to himself.

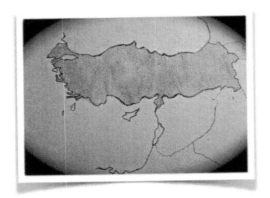

Chapter 31.

The early morning sunlight beamed onto Helen's slate grey-sided, white-trimmed three-story 1900 Colonial. An early morning breeze blew through the yard, and the leaves on the branches of the elm trees in front of her house shimmied slightly. Inside, Helen had just finished sitting at the kitchen table with a fresh cup of coffee when her doorbell rang. Nearly completely blind now, she worked her way from the kitchen and down the long hallway, feeling with her hands along the wall as she made her way toward the door. When she reached the end of the corridor, she straightened her night gown and then, grasping the door knob with both hands, she opened the door. Detective Tarsus and Adam stood on the porch.

"May I help you?" Helen asked, trying to hold a steady gaze at where she thought a person standing in the

doorway should be.

"Aunt Helen, it's me, Adam. I'm here with a police detective. May we come inside?"

"Adam. Please, come in," Helen said as she opened the front door wide. "Make your way to the sitting room, dear. I'll be with you in a moment."

Adam led Detective Tarsus down the corridor and into the first room on the left. The sitting room was very clean and simply decorated. Hardwood floors and matching crown molding framed the light pink walls in this well-lit sitting room. Pink and white flower print curtains framed the windows from floor to ceiling. The dark hand-scraped Acacia hardwood floor led the eye to the rear right of the room to a black Grand Piano. The high-gloss ebony finish and rounded corners on the Steinway indicated that this particular piano was imported from Hamburg. Along the opposite wall from the piano, there was a white couch, large enough to seat six people, resting on a plush white shag throw rug. In front of the couch, was a short coffee table made of blackened glass. Adam and Detective Tarsus sat on the couch and waited for Helen.

After a couple of minutes, Helen made her way into the sitting room and headed directly to the nearest corner of the couch and sat down. She sat the cup of coffee she had brought from the kitchen down directly in front of her on a coffee table. Adam was sitting beside her on the couch. He reached out and held her hand. Detective Tarsus rose and walked over to the piano, and stood with his hands in his pants pockets, looking down at his feet. He had given this sort of news to people before, but it never got any easier for him.

"Would either of you care for a cup of coffee or tea?" Helen asked, breaking the awkward silence. "I can have Sean pour you some if you'd like."

"No. thank you, Mrs. Morales," Detective Tarsus said. "My name is Detective Tarsus. I'm here to give you some unfortunate news concerning your son, Jordy."

"Oh my word, what's that boy done now?" Helen asked, feeling Adam's grip on her hand tightening. "Adam, what's going on?"

"Aunt Helen, something terrible has happened," Adam said in what he recognized as the bad-news voice he used when he had to give unfortunate news to the family members of deceased patients. "Jordy was shot by a man. He's dead. Uncle Pete too."

Helen began to weep heavily. Adam gave her a handkerchief from his jacket pocket.

"The man who shot your son and brother has been killed himself in an attempted burglary at your brother's house," the detective added.

"What? They were killed in an attempted burglary at Peter's house?" Helen asked. She turned her head. "Adam, I don't understand."

"We are still trying to puzzle together the pieces in this investigation," Detective Tarsus said. "I would like to offer you police protection until we figure out just what's going on."

Adam took the necklace out of his pocket and held it in his hand. He looked at it for a moment, and then he looked over at Helen. "It's about great-grandpa's necklace, Aunt Helen. He gave it to me. He asked me to keep it a secret, I'm sorry for not telling you. Jordy came over to my place to take it from me. I didn't give it to him. He chased us and this other man who was after the necklace too shot Jordy. Jordy didn't survive the gunshot. I'm sorry. Then, Uncle Pete took the necklace, and the man who shot Jordy shot Uncle Pete and Rose to get it. Rose has been taken to the hospital. I'm so sorry." He hugged his aunt.

Helen rested her head on his shoulder. Adam did not feel the wrath he anticipated receiving from her. Instead, he received from her what he sensed was failure as the matriarch of the family. She patted the young doctor's back, giving him comfort for the losses that had occurred.

Adam leaned in closer and whispered to her, "But I've

209

brought something to help you."

Helen reached out and grasped Adam's hand. When she did, she felt the necklace. "Detective, would you mind giving us a moment alone?" Helen requested politely but in a tone that would not take refusal for an answer.

"No, ma'am," Detective Tarsus said before turning his attention to Adam. "If you need me, I will be in the hall, Adam."

Adam nodded to the detective as he left the room, closing the door behind him. Adam clasped Helen's hand in both of his, closed his eyes and prayed silently. As she squeezed the silver crucifix pendant tightly, Helen began to regain her composure. The milky cloud hiding her eyes slowly began to fade, revealing her bright hazel eyes underneath. Adam's face burst into view but remained blurry as her eyes slowly regained their ability to focus.

"I knew that necklace would end up causing trouble," Helen said. "That necklace and Gramps' stupid stories drove a wedge between Peter and me. Gramps should have given it to me. I've known what to do with that thing all along. Adam, you've got to get rid of it. You've got to give it over, put it into the right hands. There's someone you need to meet. When your great-grandfather passed away, I made a call to the Vatican. I told them the story that Gramps told me many years ago about what is inside that necklace. What it really is. They sent an agent, who was expecting to get the necklace from me, but when I couldn't find the necklace, I'd thought someone had stolen it. And now that cursed thing has taken Peter and my Jordy."

Helen reached out in front of her and rang a small bell that was sitting on the coffee table next to her cup of coffee. Footsteps were immediately heard coming down the hall. Seconds later, Sean entered the sitting room.

"Sean, would you be a dear and go into the library and ask our guest to come in here?" Helen asked.

"Of course, Mother," Sean replied as he turned to retrieve their guest.

"Oh, and Sean? Did you know anything about your brother going to visit Adam's apartment to get a necklace?"

"No, Mother," Sean answered. "In fact, I haven't seen Jordy for a few days, but that's nothing new. I'll go get our guest."

"Thank you, Sean." Then Helen held her breath for a moment and tightened her grip on Adam's hands. "Adam."

"Yes, Aunt Helen."

"I can see," Helen announced with hushed astonishment. The cloudiness had faded completely from her eyes and now only the piercing hazel hue remained. Her dark pupil swirled like a drop of ink spilling onto a white page and took sharp focus on Adam's face.

"A divine miracle." A voice that Adam didn't recognize boomed across the room.

Adam turned his gaze from Aunt Helen toward the doorway. It was the mysterious man who had been following him. Adam immediately went into a cold sweat.

"Detective! Detective !" he yelled in a panic.

"Calm down, Adam," Helen snapped.

Adam leapt to his feet and took a step forward, putting himself between Helen and her mystery guest. "Aunt Helen, this is one of the men who has been chasing me. He-" Before Adam could finish his sentence, Helen cut him off.

"He is Father Vigano – from the Vatican Guard," Helen assured her nephew. She turned her attention to Father Vigano as Detective Tarsus rushed into the room with his weapon drawn. "Detective, we are all right. Father Vigano was helping me locate the necklace."

"Doctor Calhoun....Adam? Are you all right?" Detective Tarsus asked as he slowly lowered and re-holstered his weapon.

"Yes. Thanks. I'm a little jumpy, I guess," Adam replied.

"Adam, Detective, why don't you both sit down?" Father Vigano said, gesturing to the couch. "You've been through a lot," he said to Adam. "And I'm sure you both have a lot of questions you'd like answers to."

Helen stood, and Sean immediately rushed to her side and took her arm. "I'm fine, Sean," Helen said, patting her son's hand. "I'd like for you to take me to go see your brother. I'll explain along the way."

Sean nodded, not quite sure what to think of his mother's sudden ability to see or her inquiry about his brother. On their way out of the sitting room, Helen turned to Father Vigano and Adam. "I'll leave you two to talk. Adam, please—do the right thing." Then Helen walked out of the room with Sean at her side.

"Detective, if you would be so kind as to wait for us out in the hallway, I have something rather private to tell Adam. I assure you I will be most cooperative with the local law enforcement community," Father Vigano said to the amped-up detective.

Detective Tarsus looked to Adam for his cue. Adam nodded back to the detective, signaling that he would be perfectly safe alone in the room with the priest. Detective Tarsus gave a stern look of warning to Father Vigano as he marched out of the room and into the hall to wait.

"Your great-grandfather was a friend of the Church,

Adam," Father Vigano explained once they were alone. "Not only as a man of faith but he served as our official archeological consultant. Let's say that His Holiness is grateful to him for many of the items of historical significance in our collection."

"How did he become this consultant?" Adam asked.

"Your great-grandfather fought during the Great War, and was part of the Allied Invasion of Turkey in 1915, known in history books as the Battle of Gallipoli. He was there to aid in the capture of Constantinople. This proved to be a huge failure for British and French troops, and resulted in massive casualties. Your great-grandfather, a member of the Dublin Fusiliers, was one of them. Living amongst the swarms of flies feasting on rotting corpses that were swelling and bursting in the summer heat, he contracted severe dysentery. As the battle raged on, he found himself lying stranded in a sea of bodies with multiple wounds to his chest. He had been left for dead. Somehow he managed to crawl out of the battlefield where he was found by an Armenian priest, who provided him with shelter and what Henry described as the miracle of life.

"After the war, he traveled to Rome with a trunk that has been prized by the Vatican ever since...among these items was an iron nail that appeared to have had the tip filed from it. We thought it lost forever, until now."

"Papa Henry told me that he'd obtained the nail tip on a dig in Turkey in 1919. These stories don't match up."

"They never do. Sometimes you just have to make a choice as to which story you want to put your faith in."

"What happened to the Armenian priest?" Adam asked inquisitively.

"For centuries, there were rumors suggesting that Saint Helena never chopped the True Cross into pieces but that she had the two other crosses discovered at the site of the crucifixion of Christ broken up into pieces and used in place of the True Cross. The True Cross was then lost, perhaps stolen, save for the Titulus Crucis, during Helena's journey home. The Church had heard whispers about the True Cross and the Holy Nails resting, buried near a marked ossuary in Turkey. The Vatican sent a party to visit the area, and more specifically to locate Father Keshishian, the man who had healed your great-grandfather, but we were too late. By that time the Armenian Genocide was well underway and Father Keshishian was never seen from again."

"And my great-grandfather? He obviously chose to not give this to the Church," Adam said as he clutched the necklace tightly in his fist. "Why? What was his role in all of this?"

215

"Henry Calhoun was a soldier of God. He was responsible for recovering some of the Church's most revered collections. In the 1940s he stepped down, moved to America with his family, and, apart from attending Mass on Sunday, he was no longer involved in the affairs of Rome. That's about all I can tell you about Henry."

"So you're saying he was some papal Indiana Jones?"

"I'm saying the Church, the world, owes him a tremendous debt."

"I don't understand. How did he go about recovering these holy treasures?"

"In a manner befitting a soldier of the Lord. I understand your skepticism, Adam. This is an enormous amount of knowledge to process and I don't have all the answers. It would be the Vatican's wish to have the missing nail rejoined with-"

"I'm sorry, Father. I made a promise to a dying man, and I'm going to stick to my word."

Father Vigano locked his gaze upon Adam's, searching for any faltering of confidence. He did not find any. "We are living in the Year of Faith, my son." The priest took a moment to pause. "So I shall have faith in you, Dr. Calhoun. If you ever change your mind, we are only a phone call away," the priest said as he handed Adam a plain white business card with a phone number scribbled on it. "The peace of the Lord be with you always."

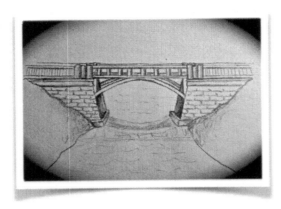

Chapter 32.

Adam and Rose strolled hand in hand through the park. The air was cool enough to warrant the jackets and scarves that they both wore without being uncomfortably cold. The sky was a bright blue with just a few fluffy white clouds hovering overhead. The branches of the tall trees, whose leaves were fully engulfed in the bright vibrant colors of fall, swayed lightly back and forth in the breeze as if they were conducting a soft secret song. Two picnickers having lunch spread out over a large blanket caught Rose's eye. She tightened her grip on Adam's hand and leaned her head on his shoulder as they walked across the beautifully maintained field. It was a perfectly beautiful fall day.

Adam stopped in his tracks as they neared the top of the small sloping hill. Something had caught his eye, something heading toward them through the trees ahead. He swept Rose behind him and stood in front of her as if to protect her. Rose looked over Adam's shoulder and saw the brown and white American Pit Bull racing toward them with its jaws open and its ID tag hanging from its collar beating against its chest with every stride. Adam turned his body and pushed Rose to the ground to shield her as the dog leapt into the air. With an arm raised in his own defense, Adam saw the dog get his prize. At the apex of the dog's leap, he met with and caught the Frisbee the dog's owner had thrown. Once the catch had been made, the dog landed and returned to his owner.

"Sorry!" the dog's owner yelled from through the trees.

Adam waved a friendly wave as he helped Rose back to her feet. The couple then walked toward the small bridge that spanned the river that split the park in two. Once they got to the middle of the bridge, Adam and Rose leaned on the south-facing rail and looked out toward the fork where the two smaller rivers joined and became one. Joggers and walkers passed behind them, enjoying the scenic trail.

"There are just too many unanswered questions," Adam said, breaking the silence and revealing to Rose what was on his mind. "I told the hospital that I'm taking an extended vacation."

"I'm going with you," Rose declared without any hint of negotiability in her voice.

Adam leaned back and looked at her for a moment. He considered a possible tactic to rebuff her statement and convince her to stay safe. She raised her eyebrows, chafed at Adam's body language.

"OK, I'm not going to argue with you on this," Adam said, realizing the futility of trying to keep Rose from joining him.

"So, where are we going?" Rose asked as she took Adam's arm in hers and snuggled into his shoulder.

"Ireland," Adam said. "And maybe a stop in Turkey."

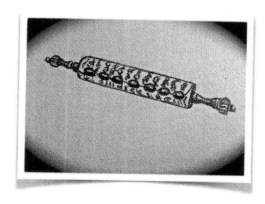

Chapter 33.

A figure wearing a white cloak was kneeling before a large wooden Latin cross attached to the wall in the chambers of a private chapel located inside a high-rise building in Chicago. The custom-made golden ring with the emblem of a slaughtered lamb resting on a scroll with seven seals made of encrusted rubies on the ring finger of his left hand revealed his identity as he prayed. Pastor Faith stood several feet behind the cloaked man.

"Sir, we are living in dangerous times," Pastor Faith began tentatively. "The rapture is close upon us. You have spoken this truth yourself. We will continue to follow your guidance, but I beg you, do not remove me from this mission."

"We will unite the people of the world under the one true God, Pastor," the cloaked figure replied, "but we must do so through peace and love. Our measures must be just and within keeping of His teachings."

"The souls of our brothers and sisters are under constant attack," Pastor Faith contended with a hint of urgency in his Southern drawl. "We are at war with the demon Satan. We must battle by wielding the sword with strength and swift resolve and cast Satan from our midst in the same manner as the archangel Michael. Please trust in me. Have faith in my methods. I will not fail you in this."

"And how did your method of violence fare in obtaining the necklace? We are too close to victory to risk tainting the greater mission. We will deliver souls into God's kingdom, but we will do so with peace and understanding. We live in trying times of temptation and desperation. God will provide us with an answer."

"The necklace is that answer. It will provide the proof for the unbelievers who require the seen in order to believe in the unseen, and strengthen the faith and resolve of all who believe. A miracle such as this is worth the sacrifice. Imagine the souls who will flock to our gates once they have witnessed the glory and healing power of God, curing the sickness within their own bodies and the bodies of others."

"Join me, Brother, in prayer."

Both men bowed their heads and recited, "And there shall be no more curse: but the throne of God and of the Lamb shall be in it; and his servants shall serve him: And they shall see his face; and his name shall be in their foreheads. And there shall be no night there; and they need no candle, neither light of the sun; for the Lord God giveth them light: and they shall reign forever and ever."

Chapter 34.

Eli stared up at the dank, off-white popcorn-style ceiling as he lay in bed. His frail body had deteriorated into a pouch that barely resembled the man he once was; a living body bag of flesh and bone. The ceiling fan above him slowly revolved, providing a gentle breeze. Eli's eyes squinted in an attempt to steady his vision as his brain tumor attacked his senses, causing double vision. The image of the fan split into two versions of itself that crossed back and forth on top of one another. As Eli slowly faded from consciousness, the gentle hum of the fan motor and the image of the spinning blades sent him into a dream-like state. The image of the rotating fan blades morphed into the twin engines on a small white gas-powered model airplane flying in the bright blue sky. A younger and healthier version of Eli watched the plane from the top of a grassy hill.

Eli closed his eyes for a moment and smiled as he felt the warmth from the sun on his face. He took a deep breath and opened his eyes. The plane circled the sky above him and dipped into a dive, heading straight for him. Eli noticed the small plane's attack run. He turned and ran down the hill in the direction of a cabin by a lake that he recognized from his childhood. The plane chased Eli down the hill, aiming its spinning blades for the back of his head. He turned and looked over his shoulder as he raced down the hill and saw the plane zooming in closer and closer. Suddenly, the small model plane crashed into the back of his head. The prop blades spun and cut into his skull, which sent searing pain through his head. Then there was blackness.

The blackness surrounded his senses until a sudden starburst of light warmed his mind. He opened his eyes and saw that he was inside the cabin. He was standing in the bathroom, looking at the claw-foot bath tub resting on a yellow and green floral laminate floor. A birch wood vanity painted white was pressed up against the wall across from the tub. A wicker basket rested on the vanity top to the left of the chrome faucet. Eli smelled the clean scent of pine and strawberry that came from the hand soap his mother would fill the basket with when he was a child. Eli inhaled deeply. A smile rose to his face. The warm calming odor of the soaps reminded Eli of his mother's face. The image that suddenly came into view was his mother when he was a young child. The tall beautiful blonde woman draped in white stood in front of Eli with her arms out as if she was reaching out to him for a welcoming embrace. Her golden blonde curls framed her smooth face. Eli focused his gaze onto her bright blue eyes. He felt a peace overcome him.

"Eli. Eli. Eli?" a distant voice repeated. At first, it was the image of his mother calling his name, but slowly the voice changed and the image of his mother began to blur. Eli slowly regained his consciousness. The haze cleared from his eyes and through it, Eli saw his best friend, Adam, standing by his side.

"Hey, buddy," Adam said gently.

"I was just dreaming about the lake house my parents used to take me to every summer," Eli said softly. "Man, that place was nice. That's where I'd like to be when I die." Eli looked at his friend Adam to ensure that his request was understood. He wanted to be taken to the lake house to die.

"We're not taking any trips today," Adam answered. "If you want to go to the lake, you'll just have to wait until summer." Adam smiled, hoping to boost his friend's morale.

"I don't think I can wait until summer. I got the MRI results."

Adam watched Eli intently, waiting for the news.

Eli slowly swallowed back a lump in his throat. "The squatter came back." He paused and took a deep breath before he continued. "And he's here to stay this time."

Adam looked up from his friend, his mind spinning a mile a second as he digested the news that Eli's cancer had returned in an advanced form. The doctor in him scrambled to find an answer.

"The doctor increased my pain meds and steroids but it looks like that's all that can be done. My dad wants me to move in with him. I don't know. Seems like a huge hassle for only a six-month lease," Eli said as he struggled to bring some levity to his situation. He took notice of Adam's silence and somber expression.

Adam took a moment and felt a heavy weight in his chest as his brain processed the information he was given. Eli was not getting better. His best friend was going to lose his battle with the tumor that had taken root within his brain. Eli had just referenced a six- month timetable, but Adam thought otherwise. Adam scanned his friend and his surroundings, and what he found sent chills through his spine. The fingers on Eli's left hand had curled into his palm, and the hand was lying in the middle of his chest. The small amount of urine that was in Eli's colostomy bag was a dark tea- colored fluid. Through their conversation, Adam noticed that Eli had been pausing more often, as if searching for the right words to say. Eli's weight loss was most likely attributed to a lack of appetite and, according to all of the signs in the room, Eli had not moved from his bed in quite some time. Adam realized that his friend most likely had two weeks to live, not the six months he thought.

Adam's hand searched his chest, grasping his great-grandfather's crucifix pendant. Papa Henry's voice echoed in his head. "When the time comes, pass this along to another deserving individual in need of healing."

The decision was made, Adam thought to himself. Eli deserves this gift. "I want you to have something of mine," Adam said as he removed the necklace from around his neck and held it out, dangling in his right hand. "This was my Papa Henry's. It's helped me through some recent difficulties, surprisingly, and I believe that it might do the same for you."

"Adam, I can't take a family heirloom from you." Eli announced at the sight of the crucifix pendant. "If Henry gave that to you—I am sure there's some historical significance."

"Eli, take it," Adam commanded persistently. There was a sharp tone in his voice that verged on the edge of panic.

"No. Why are you acting like this?" Eli was taken aback by Adam's sudden show of force.

"Look, there are a lot of things I didn't necessarily believe in anymore. But after what I've seen lately, all I can say is a lot of that has changed. So please, wear this necklace."

"Wow. Adam, am I hearing you talk about faith?"

"You're going to think I am crazy but this pendant has healing properties. It can help you, Eli. I can't get into the exact details because I don't want to put you in danger."

"In danger? I'm dying, Adam. How much more danger can I get into?" Eli laughed to himself.

"Just take it, please. This will help you get better. I know it will. I have to believe that it will." Adam found himself on the verge of desperation as he continued to plead with his friend.

Eli raised his frail shaking hand towards Adam and grasped him by the upper arm in an attempt to calm him. Tears welled up in Adam's eyes, glossing his vision as he struggled to fight back the fountain of emotion.

"Adam, I have my own." Eli gently reached under his

collar with his curled left hand and pulled out a shiny golden cross on a chain around his neck. "Remember that End of Life seminar we went to?"

Adam nodded.

"The social worker said this wasn't going to be easy on the living. I know that and I am truly sorry to you, my friends, and my dad, for putting you all through this."

"Man, you have nothing to be sorry about. But I can help," Adam assured him.

"I'm getting near my end. My fate is in God's hands, and I am okay with that. Do you hear me, Adam? I'm okay with it. You really are the greatest friend I could've asked for."

Adam leaned back slightly as he pinched his eyes and bridge of his nose with his forefinger and thumb, releasing the tear drops. Eli gently patted Adam's bicep as Adam wiped the misery from his face. After a few deep breaths, Adam looked directly at his friend and mustered a smile, nodding at Eli as he held the pendant tightly in his closed right hand.

"Can you fix my pillow? I'm getting a kink in my neck," Eli asked, trying to ease Adam's tension. He slowly rolled his neck from side to side then, with great effort, he raised his head so Adam could make the adjustment.

"You got it," Adam said quietly as he walked behind

the head of the bed to adjust Eli's pillows.

Adam helped Eli up and into a sitting position and gathered the three pillows into a tower at the head of the bed. He then quickly, without a second thought, slid his hand between the mattress and box spring at the head of the bed and put the necklace under where Eli's head would be resting. If Eli won't willingly accept the gift, Adam thought to himself, there's no reason why he still can't receive it. After depositing the pendant, Adam helped his friend lie back down.

Chapter 35.

Adam knelt before the votive candle rack inside the side sanctuary of the All Souls Catholic Church. Beams of colored sunlight shone through the stained-glass windows, illuminating the small room and bringing a vibrant realism to the statues of the Virgin Mary along with Christ on the cross within. He placed several dollars into a wooden box that rested to the side of the rack and he lit a ten-inch slow-burning match. He began to pray quietly to himself. As he spoke the words "LORD, make me an instrument of Your Peace," he lit the first candle in remembrance of his beloved mother, Mary. Adam visualized his mother as he remembered her, a smiling, loving mother where he found comfort in the soft cradle of her arms and peace in her voice and gaze. Adam continued praying. "Where there is hatred, let me sow love." He lit a second candle as he reflected on the memory of Henry, his great-grandfather who always helped guide him towards love. Next Adam reflected upon his cousin, Jordy, who had his life snuffed out too soon. "Where there is injury, pardon," Adam prayed as he lit a third candle for Jordy. "Where there is doubt, faith," Adam lit the fourth flame for his Uncle Pete.

Lastly, Adam turned his attention to the source from which he was reciting the prayer. In his left hand rested Tara's funeral prayer card that for the last ten years had occupied the corner of the frame that contained Tara's picture on his night stand. Tears gently gathered themselves up in his eyes as he recited the remainder of the prayer. "Where there is despair, hope; where there is sadness, joy." He lit the fifth candle for Tara as his mind, body and spirit was overcome with emotion. Adam felt the relief and healing release that came with expelling all of the grief, anger, and frustration that had given him such anguish in the years since Tara's death.

Adam visualized Tara as the beautiful and loving soul that he fell in love with. He realized that she was not just a memory for him to hold onto with a selfish longing that struggled daily to keep her memory frozen, trying to quell the fear of abandonment like a child afraid of releasing their mother's leg at the first sign of separation.

She was in heaven. Her spirit had and would continue to look down on him lovingly as it waited for their reunion, which would one day come, but at this moment, Adam realized she had released his physical body from his commitment to her and she would want him to continue living his life in happiness, entrusting to God's plan. He saw his mother, his great-grandfather Henry, his Uncle Pete, and his cousin Jordy all standing around Tara. His family was together, happy and content in the grace of God. The flood gates opened, and tears streamed from his eyes, drowning the flames from his vision for what seemed like minutes. Adam closed his eyes, interlaced his fingers in front of him, and continued in prayer.

After a few more moments, Adam opened his eyes and whispered, "Amen." He raised Tara's prayer card to his lips and sealed it with a kiss before placing the card on the wooden shelf in front of the candle he had lit for her. The memories of these five candles would now serve as an eternal flame of hope and faith and forgiveness for Adam. He rose to his feet and spoke in a soft voice, "Until we meet again, in a place beyond the soft blue skies, where our souls will glide and our hearts will rise, to the peace found in God's own eyes."

Rose stood beside the taxi cab near the steps leading up to the entrance of All Souls Catholic Church,

234

and watched as Adam exited the church, noticing his expression. It was sedate and calm and more at peace than she had ever seen in him. Rose took his hand in hers as he reached the taxi. They got in and the cab drove off.

The yellow-checkered Ford Crown Victoria taxi cab came to a stop at the red light. Adam gazed out the window to his right, his chin resting in the crook between his thumb and forefinger. Rose turned toward him.

"Something on your mind?" she asked, trying to break the silence.

"Something is always on my mind," Adam answered. He turned and smiled back at her. Adam shot a quick glance at the cab driver, checking to see if any attention was being paid to them at all. The cab driver appeared to be focused on the traffic light, waiting for it to turn green.

"Anything you want to share?" Rose asked. She sensed something was bothering Adam, and wished he could just open up and tell her what it was.

"Nothing special," Adam said as he took hold of her hand. "Just that I'm glad you're coming with me."

Adam was glad that Rose was going to accompany him on this journey but that wasn't the topic of conversation bouncing around inside his head. That subject was tied to his great-grandpa Henry. Specifically, the last words Henry had uttered to him the day he passed away. "Alroy Byrne" silently echoed in his mind. Adam reached into his jacket pocket and took out his one-way plane ticket to Dublin. As he stared at the ticket, ensuring its reality, questions began to race through his mind. Who was Alroy Byrne? What was so important about him that Papa Henry wanted me to know his name or seek him out? And what clues were hidden in the poem 'September 1913?'

The traffic light turned green, and with an audible sigh of relief, the driver drove the car on through the intersection toward the airport. No one in the cab noticed the silver Volkswagen Passat following them.

Chapter 36.

In St. Petersburg, Russia, the leaves also fall to the ground and the extensive parks were decorated with every shade of green, yellow, orange, red and brown. This particular year in Russia, the residents were enjoying a babe leto, or granny summer, Russia's equivalent to an Indian summer that adds an extra week or so of warmth, staving off the usual below-freezing temperatures usually felt this time of year.

Along a busy street, there was a large building surrounded by a high wall. The building was marked as The Center of Special Operations. Inside this St. Petersburg landmark, was an entire wing dedicated to the hard-working men and women of the group "Spetsnaz." On the third floor in a corner office an elderly man, dressed sharply in a starched black suit and tie, was sitting in a corner office. What little silver hair remained on top of his head was combed across the top in an attempt to hide either the baldness or the pronounced age spots that dominated his dome. His frail hands trembled as he turned the pages of the file he was reading. Suddenly, the black telephone on the corner of his desk rang.

Russian "Привет," the man said as he put the receiver to his ear. He listened intently to the person on the other end of the line, and then sharply stated, "Если розы не принимает крест, то она является предателем!" "If Rose did not take the cross, then she is a traitor!"

Chapter 37.

Adam and Rose boarded the American Airlines jet. After placing their two small suitcases into the overhead compartment, Adam sat next to Rose and buckled his seat belt. Rose finished texting a message on her phone and shut the device off, put it in her purse and wedged her purse in the seat between her and the arm rest.

"I hope you like long flights," Rose said with a smile, noticing that Adam was either nervous about flying, or already having a hard time dealing with sitting still.

"It won't be too terrible," he said, masking his fear of flying. "In three hours from now, we'll have a two-and-a-half-hour layover in Chicago, then two and a half hours after that, we'll have an almost three-hour layover in New York. Seven hours after that, and ta-da, we're in Dublin."

Suddenly, a commotion came from the front of the

plane. As the flight attendants were closing the door to the plane, a man in a dark grey overcoat, suit and tie and carrying a small travel bag shouted and pushed his way onto the plane, ticket in hand. The flight attendant checked the man's ticket then led him to an empty seat directly behind Adam and Rose. As the man walked passed Adam, they exchanged a glance that made Adam nervous. He didn't like the look of this man. Adam suspected this man could be a spy sent to follow them, or worse. Perhaps this man was sent to kill them.

Adam took Rose by the hand and squeezed, hoping she would get the signal. Just then, the flight attendant opened the overhead bin above Adam and Rose's seats and put the man's bag in the bin next to Adam's. What no one knew was that she also placed a small electronic tracking device onto the underneath side of Adam's suitcase. She closed the bin and took her preflight position. Adam and Rose sat holding hands as the plane taxied its way to the take-off point of the runway, marking the beginning of their next big adventure.

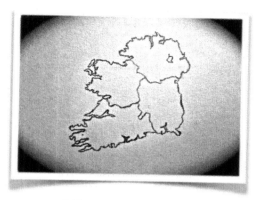

Chapter 38.

All will be revealed in thy neighbor's grave.

The year was 1894; the place was a small village in County Clare, Ireland. Maeve Byrne hollered in pain as she clutched the wooden edge of the bed she was propped up on to deliver her child. She was a young woman of sixteen, nearly seventeen, with dark black curly hair, bright emerald eyes and soft facial features that were covered in the grime of a poorer, labor-filled life. Maeve's curly black hair sank against her neck and shoulders, damp with sweat, and streaks of dirt ran down her face like a mudslide as her face contorted in pain, pushing through another severe contraction. Her voice changed from a helpless scream of pain into a deep guttural yell of determination as she pushed.

The midwife's eyes lit up. She thrust her hands

forward, gripped the newborn by the head and shoulders and carefully but firmly pulled the child into the unfamiliar elements of the world. Maeve's voice exhaled and fell silent, exhausted. A cry broke the silence as the midwife cleaned the newborn's airways and placed the tiny gift of life onto Maeve's chest, skin to skin. Maeve looked upon the child in wonderment and a feeling of unconditional love that can only be understood through the experience of childbirth. Her world would forever be changed, and yet time seemed to hold still. She felt as if her child had always been a part of her life, even though the little boy had been placed in her arms moments earlier. Maeve wept tears of joy as she looked upon the boy's delicate face as he stretched his tiny hands and clasped his fingers to her garments.

"What are you going to call him?" whispered the midwife.

"My little Alroy. Alroy Byrne." Maeve gently kissed the boy's forehead as they rested comfortably. The bond between mother and child was now completely forged between them. Maeve was so infatuated with her little boy and exhausted from the ordeal that she barely noticed the afterbirth pains. Baby Alroy nuzzled his mother's chest as he began to purse his lips and suckle at the air.

"He's hungry," the midwife said with a wistful smile.

The wrinkles crinkled across her face in a burst of joy at the beauty of new life.

As Maeve went to nurse the child, there was a sudden pounding coming from the other room. Terror overcame the midwife, who bolted for the window in order to flee the scene. The midwife climbed out of the window and motioned for Maeve to follow suit.

"Come, Maeve. Now. Hurry. It's the Order. They found us," the midwife said as her pupils burst in fright.

The fervor of the pounding on the door grew. The sounds of boots thumped the wooden barrier that shielded her from the hallway. Maeve gathered her son in her arms and strained to push herself off the bed, but it was too late. Maeve froze as the door to the room flew open and wood splinters exploded into the air.

The midwife disappeared from view, leaving Maeve and her baby Alroy to the horrors that awaited them. Several men rushed into the room and took hold of Maeve by her wrists and legs as a nun from the local convent gently but quickly swept up the baby in her arms. Maeve and her innocent child were abducted from their home and hauled off into the darkness toward an unknown future.

ABOUT THE AUTHORS

James Stevenson

James Stevenson was born and raised in Hannibal, Missouri. He was catholic schooled from the first through the seventh grades. James joined the U.S. Navy in 1988 and served until 1992. He now resides in Los Angeles, California where he works as an actor under the stage name Dallas James. *The Iron Relic* is James' first book.

Bobby Hundley

Bobby Hundley has always had a fascination with history, archeology and medicine which made *The Iron Relic* a true passion piece for him. As a child, he grew up hearing stories of miraculous healings from his own Papa, who was a strong man of faith. He now resides in Los Angeles, California where he works as a producer, writer and actor. Bobby serves as the Producing Artistic Director of the San Gabriel Valley Music Theatre and co-director of the Arcángel Film Festival. He has a children's book series: *The Adventures of Princess Lainey* coming out in 2015.

To learn more about The Iron Relic Book Series, please visit us on the World Wide Web at

www.theironrelicbook.com

Class one — set expectations

Read Chapter I together

Workshop readings Chapters

1   37

1   2   3   4   5   6 | pages 20 page

6   7   8   9   10 | pages 21

10 11   12   13   14 | pages 22

14 15   16   17   18 | pages 31

18 19   20   21   22 | pages 31

22 23   24   25   26 | pages 22

26 27   28   29   30 | pages 28

30 31   32   33 | pages 4 x 9 = 36

34   35   36   37